JUST
YOUR
EVERYDAY
PEOPLE

Novels by Fred Yager and Jan Yager
Untimely Death

Selected Nonfiction Books by Jan Yager (www.janyager.com)
(a/k/a J.L. Barkas)
Victims
Friendshifts®: The Power of Friendship and How It Shapes
    Our Lives
Business Protocol
Creative Time Management for the New Millennium
Effective Business and Nonfiction Writing

JUST YOUR EVERYDAY PEOPLE

a novel

Fred Yager
Jan Yager

HANNACROIX CREEK BOOKS, INC.
Stamford, Connecticut

Dedicated to our wonderful sons, Scott and Jeffrey

Copyright © 2001 by Fred Yager and Jan Yager
Cover photograph by Fred Yager

LCCN: 00-134588

Publisher's Cataloging-in-Publication *(Provided by Quality Books, Inc.)*

Yager, Fred, 1946-
   Just your everyday people: a novel / Fred Yager, Jan Yager. – 1st ed.
   p. cm.
   ISBN: 1-889262-17-X

   I. Yager, Jan, 1948 - II. Title.
   PS3575.A447E94 2001   813'.54
                          QBI00-901469

Published by:
Hannacroix Creek Books, Inc.
1127 High Ridge Road, PMB 110
Stamford, CT 06905-1203
e-mail: Hannacroix@aol.com
URL: http://www.Hannacroix.com

1

SHE COULD see it in his eyes, the pleading, the fear, the pain, and the terror. This one was a real bleeder, too. Splatters of dark red spread out in every direction from the opening.

"Please. No more," he begged, only it sounded like *preeze no ma.*

His eyes filled with tears and for a moment, no longer than a heartbeat, she nearly considered stopping. But she knew it was better to keep going, to just get it done. He looked up again, his anxious eyes trying to connect with hers. She refused to look back, focusing her attention on the task at hand. She was a professional with a job to do. She knew that to submit to his pleading would do him more harm than good.

Julia never thought of herself as a cruel person, yet the punishment she was being forced to inflict made her feel that way. As she pushed the blood-covered instrument deeper into his flesh, she could feel the man's pain. Her mentor once told her that it was this kind of empathy that would set her apart from most of the others in her field. But then she looked down at the anguish in his eyes and it almost broke her heart. Why should she feel such overwhelming pity? If he had only done what he was supposed to do, this wouldn't be happening. In fact, this whole bloody mess was *his* fault.

She paused to wipe away some blood, then shifted her angle and was about to push in deeper when he grabbed her wrist and cried out, "No! No more!"

Julia lowered her head in surrender. She couldn't continue and that made her feel worse because aborting the process now would result in severe consequences. She put down her instrument and let out a deep breath.

"Mr. Blackson. If I stop now, you're gonna lose those back molars. I don't like this anymore than you do. Believe me. It hurts me to see you in such pain. But you're not flossing. Which means all the tartar is building up between your teeth and around your gums. Do you want to have periodontal work? If you think this hurts, wait until some oral surgeon starts to cut into your jaw for a bone graft. So, please Mr. Blackson, let me finish. We're almost done. But if we stop now, you'll just have to come back in a week so I can finish. What do you say? We can do this. I'll go as slow as I can to ease the pain. If it hurts, just raise your hand and I'll stop, okay?

"Here, why don't you rinse out before we continue," she said, handing him a small paper cup filled with water and diluted mint-flavored green mouthwash.

"We're really almost done?" he asked after spitting water, blood, and plaque into the bright white enamel basin next to the chair.

"Fifteen more minutes. Tops. I just have to clean the back molars and the upper left quadrant. You've got beautiful teeth, Mr. Blackson. Why don't we see what we can do to save them?"

"If I raise my hand, you promise you'll stop?"

"I promise." She picked up the silver scaler and started toward a back molar. Up went a hand. She stopped and straightened up. "Mr. Blackson. I didn't even touch you."

"Just testing."

"I'll be as tender as I can," said Julia, smiling.

This time, she leaned in closer, letting her upper body press against him until she could feel her left breast softly brush against his cheek. It was a maneuver she had perfected in the years after oral hygienist school. It always had the same soothing effect on male and female patients, similar to that of a masseuse whose trained touch could calm while carefully arouse the deepest erotic fantasies. It worked better than a shot of novocaine. As she scraped deeper below the swollen, sensitive gum line, she looked down at Harry Blackson's face, which earlier had been a contortion of pain. He now looked content, lost in far away thoughts, comforted by the warmth of the connection with her. He didn't raise his hand even once.

Twenty minutes later, Julia put down her instrument and removed the soft rubber-covered saliva ejector from Harry Blackson's mouth.

"All done," she said. "I think maybe you should see me again in four months instead of six."

"So soon?"

"One of the reasons this hurt so much is because it's been almost a year since your last cleaning. You should come in every four months. If you do that, it won't hurt at all."

Harry Blackson looked like he was in a daze as he lifted himself out of the chair. Julia gave him another cup of mouthwash, which he took gratefully.

"Nina will make another appointment for you."

He washed out his mouth and handed the cup back to Julia. She sensed that he wanted to say something.

"Are you all right, Mr. Blackson?"

"Huh. I'm fine."

"I know this was hard, but you did great. Your gums are gonna be a little sore and sensitive to cold for a few hours. We have to close up now. So make that appointment, okay? I'll see you in four months."

She looked at her watch. It was 6:20 and she was supposed to meet her husband and their friends five minutes ago. But Harry wasn't leaving. It wasn't the first time this had happened. Especially after a grueling session, like this had been. Some patients seemed to form a kind of bond with her that took a little extra effort to break. Julia learned that one of the most effective methods was to involve the patient in her cleanup activity.

"If you're going to stand there, would you mind handing me that tray?" she said, nodding toward a tray of bloody cotton swabs and instruments.

Harry took one look at the carnage that had come from his mouth and backed toward the door of the tiny room.

"I just realized, I'm supposed to be somewhere else right now. Gotta go," he blurted out as he dashed through the doorway.

After washing the trays and wiping down the chair, Julia put her cleaning instruments into a clear plastic bag that would be collected by a sterilization service. She was taking one last look around the office when her pager vibrated against her hip. Julia reached into the pocket of her tight white uniform and pulled out the black plastic rectangular device. The message was from her husband Paul. They were all at The Ostrich drinking, where was she?

According to the clock in the reception area, it was now almost 6:30. Julia waved goodnight to Nina, grabbed her green canvas tote bag, a freebie from a dental trade show, and headed out the door. By the time she got to her car, the beeper was vibrating again. This time the message was "We're hungry so we're ordering some nachos. I'll try to save you some." Julia smiled as she put her pager away. They'd been married for five years but they still acted like newlyweds, spending as much time together as possible, and then getting worried and protective when one wasn't where he or she was supposed to be, like now.

Julia got behind the wheel of their 1982 Buick Skylark, pushed a Tom Petty cassette into the tape player and pulled out of the parking lot singing along "I'm free, free falling ...."

The downtown traffic was typical for a "TGIF" Friday night as office workers and commuters celebrated the end of another week by driving to their favorite local bar.

Normally, Julia would have already joined her husband and their best friends since high school, Lizzie and John. But this last cleaning had taken longer than usual. She estimated she was about three drinks behind them already. So instead of going home to change, she pulled into the self-service island at the combination gas station and convenience store where she bought coffee on the way to work each morning.

She parked the car, which had been a gift from her parents, next to the 87-octane pump and got out. Julia figured the car would last another year at the most, even though it was still going strong with 167,000 hard miles on the odometer.

She set the latch on the gas pump so it would continue filling, grabbed her tote bag from the back seat and went inside the convenience store to use the ladies' room. Fortunately, she had the room to herself, so she locked the door and stripped off the starched white dental hygienist uniform. Looking into the mirror, she could see the red lines where the tightness of the stiff cotton had cut into skin. Time to go back on a diet. No nachos tonight.

Julia got out her compact, even though she had the kind of face that didn't need much makeup. While she'd never been the most beautiful girl in school, she had a natural attractiveness, with deep blue eyes, shoulder length natural blonde hair, and a smile that seemed to promise wonderful things to come. At 28, she had to work harder to keep in shape, so she did aerobic and weight exercises three nights a week at the downtown Y. Even that hadn't been enough to stop the ten extra pounds that seemed to creep up on her from no where. At first she thought that maybe she was finally pregnant, since she and Paul had been trying to have a baby for the past four years. But the arrival of her period squashed that dream. It was the donuts Dr. Jacobs had been bringing in. The freshly-baked glazed donuts were definitely addictive. She was just going to have to force herself to treat them like any other controlled substance and just say "no."

She put on a tiny dab of dark red lipstick and some black eyeliner, then reached into her tote and pulled out an embroidered denim shirt, a short fringed brown suede skirt, a leather vest, and knee-high black leather boots. Paul liked it when she dressed like a cowgirl. She had almost packed a white cowboy hat, but decided that would be overkill.

She checked her watch. Seven o'clock. At least the nachos would be gone. She checked her pager. Fifteen minutes had gone by and Paul hadn't called. He's probably flirting with that waitress, Darlene.

2

THERE WERE other places they could go in Lakeside, Connecticut, a mostly commuter town of 77,000 about forty-five minutes northeast of Manhattan. There were other restaurants that served better food, other bars that catered to a fancier crowd and stocked pricier liquors. But over the years, the Ostrich had become *their* place. It was where they went to smooth out the knots and torment of a week of imprisonment at their tedious and monotonous jobs. It was their oasis in a desert of disappointment that had fallen over each of their lives as the hopes and dreams of their youth slowly transformed into the realization that this might be as good as it would ever get.

They would meet at the Ostrich on Friday nights after work to reward themselves for surviving another week of self-imposed confinement in their minimum-security jobs.

Julia parked in the back lot since the front was already full.

From the outside, The Ostrich looked like the grain warehouse it used to be. The faded paint on the original brick siding proclaimed the finest barley, wheat, corn, and hops. But now the only hops were in the domestic and imported beers available by bottle or draft.

Julia stepped inside and saluted its namesake, a giant stuffed ostrich with its head buried in a pitcher of beer mounted on the wall behind the bar.

Only 7:15 and the place was already filling up. Couples were dancing on the tiny sawdust-covered floor in the back. Singles were hanging out around the bar, holding on to the edges of high wooden stools. Julia had to push her way through the intense crowd, declining several offers of drinks and even one marriage proposal from Luke. He was one of the Friday night regulars, a baby-faced generation-x bond trader who had relocated from Silicon Valley to the new investment bank that had just opened up downtown. Every Friday night for the past two months, Luke had proposed; and every Friday night, Julia turned him down.

Moving farther into the darkness of the bar, Julia felt a strange sensation, as if the ordinary craziness of end of the week ribaldry was starting earlier, making way for an even more bizarre evening. There seemed to be more strangers here tonight, businessmen in town for a convention or a national sales meeting. For the first time in as long as she could remember, the strangers outnumbered the regulars.

From the thick layer of cigarette smoke, Julia wondered if the Surgeon General's warning had been dismissed as a cruel hoax. Mixed with the aroma of smoke was the blended scents of beer and barbecue, perfume and sweat, the smell of the hunt.

She finally made it past the gauntlet at the bar and was walking among the dancing couples when she spotted them crammed into a booth against the back wall.

"Call off the missing persons," shouted Paul Stanton loud enough for half the room to hear. "We thought we lost you for sure. Did you get my beeps?"

At 31, Paul Stanton looked like he was still in high school. Tall and thin, with a crooked smile and sandy brown hair that hung down over his forehead, he still weighed what he had weighed at graduation. He could eat a two-foot long platter of short ribs and half a chicken—all drowning in barbecue sauce, extra fries and butter-soaked corn on the cob—and not gain an ounce. It made Julia furious, since all she had to do was look at a carbohydrate to become bloated. Paul was still wearing his bluish green service station shirt with his name embroidered over the left pocket.

"Sorry I'm late," said Julia, sliding into the booth. "Are they giving away free drinks tonight? I don't think I've ever seen it this crowded."

"It's that new on-line securities firm that opened up downtown," said Paul. "Six thousand traders and investment bankers. Supposed to help property values, but it's also made getting around town twenty times harder."

"There a rodeo in town, darlin?" asked Lizzie, giving Julia's western attire the once over.

Julia felt as if she'd been slapped. "You don't like it?"

Lizzie was wearing a short leather mini-skirt with a low cut, almost see-through black blouse. She reached across the table and put her hand on Julia's. "Are you kidding? I love it. I'm just jealous I didn't think of something like that. But then I don't think I'd be able to pull off the Annie Oakley look. Calamity Jane maybe."

"Well, I think she looks wonderful," Paul said, smiling, then giving his wife a kiss on the mouth. "I don't know how you do it, baby. We both work hard all day but you still manage to look like a movie star."

"Hey Julia," said Lizzie's husband John, a dark, handsome man with thick black eyebrows and big brown eyes that always looked surprised. "We got some rope out in the Jeep. Maybe we could play lasso the steer later."

Lizzie turned toward her husband and reached under the table. "I don't think that's necessary. In fact, I believe I have one of the steer's horns right here."

"Ouch! Take it easy, honey."

"Say you're sorry," demanded Lizzie.

"I'm sorry. Jesus! Julia knew I was just kidding. Can we order some food now? Damn that hurt."

"There, there, baby," said Lizzie giving her husband a kiss on his cheek, while giving Julia a wink. "He's been tossing back shots since he got here. I think it's time to switch to beer, honey. Where's that waitress? We should probably order. The sooner he gets some food in him, the better we'll all be."

"There she is," said Paul. "Hey, Darlene. We're ready to order some food."

A well-endowed waitress with a plastic nameplate that said "Darlene" pinned over her left pocket arrived, flipped open an order pad and smiled down at Paul.

"What are you all having?" asked Darlene.

Julia ordered a Cobb salad with light-style ranch dressing, while Paul went for his usual chicken and ribs.

Lizzie said she wanted prime rib, rare and John got a rack of barbecued baby backs.

"Why doncha bring us another round, too?" asked Paul, grinning up at the waitress.

"Let's see," said Darlene. "That's two beers, a frozen margarita and, what's that thing you always order?" She looked at Julia for a second. "A vodka martini. No ice."

"Darlene, you're a regular walkin' encyclopedia," said Paul."

10

Darlene winked at Paul, closed her pad, and ambled away. Julia could feel her face redden as she glared at Paul.

"What?" said Paul, sheepishly. "It's just Darlene."

"Hey cowgirl, let's check out the ladies' room," said Lizzie.

Julia and Lizzie had been best friends since ninth grade. Back then, Lizzie was the prettier of the two. They were 14 and Julia was going through an awkward phase, thirty extra pounds, and big red patches of acne. But in their 20s, things changed and Julia lost her baby fat, her face cleared up, and her once pudgy cheeks flattened as she blossomed into a natural beauty that seemed to get prettier every year. Not that Lizzie wasn't nice to look at. She was. She also had a seductiveness about her that attracted men like flies to sticky sugar on a hot summer night. Julia often wondered how John put up with men coming on to his wife all the time, but Lizzie had confided to her one night that he didn't mind because it got him excited. Julia wondered if Paul felt that way about her. John, while two inches shorter than Lizzie, was actually more handsome than Lizzie was pretty. That didn't bother Lizzie. In fact, she liked having a good-looking husband. He was her trophy.

Once inside the ladies room, Lizzie took out a filtered cigarette and lit it up.

"I thought you quit," said Julia.

"I did," said Lizzie, taking a deep drag. "How are you and Paul doin?"

"Whatta ya mean?"

"You know. Trying to get pregnant. You still taking that fertility stuff?"

"No. Somebody told me it might bring on early menopause."

"You could do a lot better, ya know."

"What's that supposed to mean?"

11

"You know what I mean. I'm not saying Paul's not a nice guy. He is. He's just, I don't know, boring."

"Maybe I like boring."

"All I know is that you could do a lot better."

"You're starting to sound like my mother. It just so happens that I love him."

"What are you gonna do if it turns out he doesn't have any bullets in the chamber? All the fertility drugs in the world ain't gonna help you then."

"We had him tested and he's fine. We both are. The doctor said it's up to God and timing. When it's the right time, I'll get pregnant."

"If you want a kid so bad, you can have mine," said Lizzie, taking another drag.

"You don't mean that."

"I know. Hell, Brian's the best thing that ever happened to me. But raising kids isn't as easy as you think. They take over your life."

"You're here, aren't you? Who's watching Brian tonight?"

"My grandmother."

"Sounds like you got things under control."

"Oh yeah. We got things under control. We're two months overdue on our mortgage. John's carpentry work has slowed to a crawl. Tips at the beauty parlor are half what they were last year and Hector's cut back my hours at the diner. Things are just great."

"Why didn't you say something. I've got a little money saved up," said Julia, "if you wanta borrow some."

"You got an extra thirty-five thousand lying around?"

"I was thinking more like a couple hundred. What happened?"

"We got a little carried away in the credit card department. I mean they keep sending us applications all the time. Before we knew it, we were paying over a thousand dollars a month to the credit card companies. For a while, we were using one credit card to pay for another and it just piled up. Then we went to one of those home equity places, but when we missed one payment, they threatened to take our house away. So I went to Eddie the Hand for a bridge loan. Just to tide us over. John was supposed to get this job working on the renovation of a movie theater across from the new campus, but it went to a different contractor and he don't like John."

"Eddie the Hand? What were you thinking? At least with the credit cards, if you can't pay the bill, they just cut up your card, not your face. What are you gonna do?"

"We'll figure something out." Lizzie took another deep drag of her cigarette and looked at Julia's feet. "Those boots look familiar."

"They should," said Julia, looking down. "You loaned them to me in eleventh grade, remember? I tried to give them back when we were seniors but they didn't fit you anymore so you told me to keep them."

"Oh yeah," said Lizzie, taking a final drag on the cigarette before grinding it out on the bathroom floor. "If I tell you something, will you promise to keep it a secret?"

"You know I will."

"John can't get it up any more."

"Do I really want to hear about this?"

"I gotta tell somebody. Remember when I told you he could only get excited when he saw another man comin' on to me?"

"Yeah."

"Well, lately, it hasn't been working. I even brought another woman home one night. That's been one of his all-time favorite fantasies, ya know, me and another woman."

"Lizzie! You really did that?"

"I was getting worried about him, but even that didn't work. We got an appointment at the family planning clinic next Monday, see if we can get us some of that Viagra."

"How long has this been going on?"

13

"Couple of months. I think it's the money thing. He can't support the family so he can't perform."

"How are you holding up?"

"I'm okay. It just breaks my heart seeing him like that. Sometimes I get the feeling he wished I'd go off with someone else, just to take some of the pressure off him."

"Would you do that?"

"I don't know. It's pretty tempting. I can almost see myself going out there, cutting one of them cute young turks away from the herd. Do a little dirty dancing."

"If you do, ask Luke," said Julia. "I don't think he's been with a woman since he moved here."

That got them both laughing so hard, Lizzie knocked her red purse off the sink, spilling its contents across the linoleum floor. Julia knelt down to help when she noticed the gun. It was lying there amidst the compact, lipstick, green hairbrush, and keys, a silver automatic 22-caliber handgun. Lizzie quickly pushed everything back into her purse and looked at Julia.

"John gave it to me for Valentine's Day."

"How romantic."

"I asked him to get me one. For when I have to work late at the diner. It's not in the best neighborhood you know."

"Maybe we should get back in there before Darlene puts the moves on Paul," said Julia.

"It's way too late, honey." Lizzie smiled. "She started sticking her tits in his face the minute he sat down. If you hadn't shown up when you did, I was gettin ready to dump a beer on his head just to cool him off."

3

BY THE TIME they returned to the booth, their food and next round of drinks had arrived. Julia devoured her salad and wished she'd ordered something more filling. As she ate, she thought about what Lizzie had said about her husband. She looked at Paul and felt a pang of sadness. While neither had achieved their dreams—his of finishing college and owning his own business, or hers of having a baby and going to dental school and becoming an oral surgeon—she still felt that she made the right choice for a husband.

But as she looked around the crowded bar, she wondered if this was as good as it was ever going to get for them. Work all week and then drink themselves into oblivion on the weekend? She was sure that a child would help. It would give their lives meaning. But then she looked at Lizzie and John. They had a kid, and where were they? Thirty-five thousand dollars in debt to a loan shark who used to sit behind them in homeroom making obscene noises and gestures just to piss off the teacher.

Eddie Espisito was always looking to lend you a hand, hence the name "Eddie the Hand." He was forever getting into trouble in school, smoking in the boys' room, talking back to teachers, but he never got expelled. Julia learned later that the reason he was allowed to stay was because his family was connected; one night, the principal received a call after one of Eddie's many suspensions for swearing in the classroom. No one ever found out who made the call, or what was said, but from then on, the teachers left Eddie alone, even though he never toned down his act. He'd still tease a student now and then but usually he left teachers alone. It was obvious that a deal had been struck and the word spread that Eddie was someone to steer clear of. He didn't scare Lizzie, though. She used to flirt with him until one day he asked her out and she just laughed at him. The next afternoon, he pulled out a knife and forced her into the girls' room. He pushed her into a stall and started to unzip his jeans when they heard a toilet flush two stalls down. The stall door opened and out stepped Mrs. Hoskins, the language arts teacher.

Lizzie waited until Mrs. Hoskins was at the sink until she reached behind Eddie and flushed, then stepped out of the stall, closing the door behind her, before Mrs. Hoskins could see into the stall. Lizzie nodded to the teacher and then went to another sink. She quickly washed her hands and then left the girls' room right behind Mrs. Hoskins. The next day in homeroom, Eddie leaned over next to Lizzie and whispered that he owed her one and that if she ever needed anything to let him know. Apparently, Lizzie had finally taken Eddie up on his offer.

Darlene returned and took their plates away, then came back with another round of drinks. She started to lean into Paul when she saw the icy stare from Julia and backed away.

It was nearly nine o'clock and the crowd at the bar had grown to capacity. Jake the doorman was turning people away and a line had formed at the front door and stretched halfway down the block. Whenever anyone left, Jake would let someone in.

An up-tempo R&B song from the 60s was playing on the jukebox as the dance floor filled with couples. Lizzie tried to pull John up to dance, but he could barely stand. She let him fall back into the booth, then reached out to Julia. "Come on, darlin. Let's show these boys how it's done."

Julia let herself be pulled out of the booth and on to the dance floor. It was a fast dance, and she and Lizzie blended into the writhing, jerking bodies, moving in time with the syncopated rhythm. Every now and then, Lizzie would wiggle up against her and then playfully move away. Julia glanced at the booth and saw John and Paul both watching them. She motioned for Paul to join them but he shook his head "no."

She looked back at Lizzie and noticed her friend was staring off toward the bar. Julia turned her head slightly to follow Lizzie's line of sight.

He was wearing a gray pinstriped suit with a red and blue paisley tie loosened at the neck. His dark brown hair, with streaks of gray, was combed to the side in a somewhat disheveled way. There was an "I just don't give a damn" expression on his boyishly handsome face. His soulful eyes were locked on Lizzie's.

The Stranger finished his drink in one gulp, turned away, and ordered another round with the wave of his hand.

Lizzie used the occasion to look over at her husband who was staring right back at her. John then looked toward the bar where the man stood and then back toward Lizzie. Julia could see a look pass between them, an acknowledgement. John lifted his bottle and drained it. It took a moment before Julia realized the song had ended and that another was about to start. Lizzie kissed Julia on the cheek, squeezed her hand, and then started to walk toward the bar.

Julia stood there watching as Lizzie slithered to the bar and wedged herself in between the man and another woman who was about to make a move. Lizzie gave the other woman a look that said she was prepared to cut out her heart if necessary. The other woman backed away as Lizzie pressed up against the Stranger who now had his back to her. He turned around and looked down the front of Lizzie's blouse, seeing the upper most half moons of her nipples.

"Lookin for something?" she said, smiling.

The Stranger looked up at Lizzie's face and blinked. He then raised the glass to his lips and drank the brown liquid over ice while looking across the room to see John staring right back at him from the booth in back.

"You wanta dance?" asked Lizzie, smiling seductively. "I don't think so."

"Why not?"

"There's a guy over there looking at me for one."

"That's just my husband. He won't mind."

"You sure about that?"

"We have an arrangement."

"What kind of arrangement?"

"We can pretty much fool around with anybody we want as long as we go home together."

"And is that what you're doing? Fooling around?

"I guess that depends on you."

The Stranger looked over at John and saw him staring back at him. John didn't look too happy.

"I think maybe you should go back to your husband."

"What if I don't want to?"

"It's a free country," said the Stranger, turning back to his drink.

Lizzie looked at John who moved his head side to side lightly, but the message was clear. "Stop." But this guy was perfect, thought Lizzie. He was wearing a wedding band. His suit was tailor-made. He was exactly what they'd been looking for. This was their ticket to financial freedom. Now it looked like John was getting cold feet. Well, it was too late. This guy was ready to go. She could smell it.

"Come on," she said, putting her hand on his arm. "Dance with me."

"I don't think so."

"You're not afraid of me, are you?"

"Should I be?"

"A big strong man like you."

"I just don't want any trouble with your husband over there."

"He's not gonna give you any trouble." Lizzie took the Stranger's hand and led him reluctantly to the dance floor. Elton John's "Someone Saved My Life Tonight" was playing. Lizzie pressed up against the Stranger's hard body. He was tall, about six-four, and Lizzie's head came up to his chest.

As they moved around the floor, Julia returned to the booth and sat down next to Paul who, along with John, was watching Lizzie and the Stranger.

"Hey, John, who's that dancing with Lizzie?" asked Paul.

John turned to look at Paul and then looked at Julia. He just stared at her for a beat and then turned back toward the dance floor.

"Did I say something wrong?" asked Paul.

"It's probably somebody she knows from the diner," said Julia, as she looked at John staring at his wife dancing with the Stranger. There was pain in his eyes and Julia felt frustrated over not knowing how to deal with the situation.

She was torn between her loyalty to Lizzie and hating what she was doing to her husband.

On the dance floor, Lizzie looked like she was in a dream as she melted against the Stranger. She could feel him getting aroused as she pushed her breasts and hips into him. She reached up and touched his cheek. There was a look of sadness around his eyes that triggered in Lizzie a maternal desire to comfort his pain. Maybe this wasn't such a good idea. Something was going on inside this guy. Maybe that's what John had picked up on. She needed more information.

"Let's go outside," she whispered, "get some air?"

John watched them leave, then turned toward Paul and Julia. "How about one more round," he said, smiling, although his eyes were red. "Where's Darlene? Darlene! Get over here."

"Maybe we ought to call it night," said Paul.

"Yeah," added Julia. "I've got a go to the office tomorrow for an emergency root canal."

"You're not gonna leave me here to drink alone, are you?"

"We'd never do that," said Paul. "I just figured…"

"Don't worry about Lizzie. She can take care of herself."

"It's not Lizzie we're worried about, John," said Julia.

"What? Me? I'm fine. I just need another drink," said John. "I've also gotta use the men's room. Just order us one more round. I really need it. Then we'll go. Okay?"

The rear door of the Ostrich opened and Lizzie stepped out, dragging the Stranger behind her by his tie. As soon as the door closed behind them, she turned into him and tilted her head up. They started to kiss with abandon, their body temperatures rising as his tongue filled her mouth.

Catching her breath, Lizzie pulled away and leaned against a wooden railing on the rear deck. "Do you have a car?" she asked.

Without speaking, he led her to a new white top-of-the-line Lexus with New York plates. He took out a plastic remote security device and pressed a button. The car beeped and he opened the back door on the driver's side.

She climbed in first, feeling the soft leather seats with her hands as she slid across to make room. Yes, she thought. This guy has money.

As soon as he got in, he pressed the button on the plastic remote and the doors locked again.

"Why'd you lock the doors?" she said.

"Just a precaution."

"So," said Lizzie. "How come I've never seen you here before?"

"I'm just passing through."

"Passing through to where?"

"What are we gonna do here, play twenty questions?"

Lizzie answered by putting her mouth over his, then straddling him. She clawed at his shirt and pulled off his tie. He tore open her blouse and cupped a breast in each hand. He then slid down to take a nipple in his mouth when suddenly a bright cone of light filled the car. He looked stunned as Lizzie took his head and kissed him, pushing her tongue into his mouth as the light moved up and down their bodies. Although he could feel himself growing more excited, the light was troubling. He pulled away from Lizzie and turned toward the direction of the light.

"What the hell?" shouted the Stranger.

"Just take it easy," said Lizzie, trying to straighten her blouse to cover herself as she got off him and moved to the far side of the back seat.

The Stranger was looking around, confused.

"Somebody's out there," he said.

"It's just my husband."

"What is this, a robbery? What was that light?"

"He's making a video."

"A video?"

"Okay. Here's the deal. We're gonna help you get out of trouble with your wife."

"You know about my wife?"

"We're going to sell you the video for, let's say $50,000. If you don't want to buy the tape of you sucking my tit, we're going to send it overnight express to your wife. We have your license plate number, which is all I need for my friend at the DMV to get me your address."

The Stranger stared at Lizzie for a second and then a smile slowly formed on his face.

"What's so funny?"

"Life," he replied. "Life is funny."

"Lizzie?" It was John. He tapped on the window. "Is everything okay in there?"

"Everything's fine," said Lizzie. "So, how do you want to do this?"

"Do what?" asked the Stranger.

"Get us $50,000."

"Well, ya see, that's the funny part. What do we have in here?" he said as he grabbed Lizzie's purse.

"What are you doing?"

"Well, you've got a friend at the DMV to find out who I am. I'd like to know who I'm dealing with as well."

"Give me that," she said making a swipe, but he snapped it away before she could get it, causing the leather top of her red purse to flop open and the contents to fly out all over the seat. They both looked down at the same time to see the silver handgun sitting among the metal tubes of lipstick, green hairbrush, compact and keys. The Stranger beat her to it.

John pounded on the car. "Lizzie, are you all right?"

"John! He's got my gun!" shouted Lizzie.

"Get out of there, Lizzie!" yelled John.

She reached for the door nearest her, but it was still locked. "The doors are locked." She turned to the Stranger who was pointing the gun at her. "Okay. You win. John. I blew it. Give him the tape."

"Not until you're out of there."

The Stranger examined the small pistol.

"We don't know what the hell we're doing, mister. We're just a couple of desperate people about to have our house repossessed by a bank and our legs broke by a pissed-off loan shark. I got a five-year-old boy who has to wear our neighbor's son's clothes to school because we can't afford to buy him his own. We got scared and did something dumb. Haven't you ever been so scared, you didn't know what to do, so you did something really stupid?"

The Stranger looked up from the gun and stared at her.

"So, why don't we just forget this whole thing. You let me out, and my husband will give you the video and we can just go on with our miserable lives."

The Stranger responded by pushing a lever between the two front bucket seats. The driver's seat tilted back, allowing the Stranger enough room to climb into front seat behind the steering wheel. He pressed the lever again and the seat back returned to its upright position.

"What are you doing?" asked Lizzie.

"Lizzie! What's going on?" yelled John as he heard the car's engine come on.

"John. Get me out of here!"

The car lurched back out of its parking space, throwing Lizzie forward against the back of the front passenger seat. The front tires spun into the gravel as the Stranger shifted gears. Just before the wheels gained traction, John leaped onto the hood.

"Stop the car," John yelled.

The Stranger pushed down on the accelerator and the car sped out of the parking lot with John holding on for his life. Just before the car reached the highway, the Stranger made a sharp right turn and slammed on the brakes. John went flying over the left front bumper and onto a grassy bank. The Stranger hit the gas pedal again and peeled rubber down the highway.

"John!" screamed Lizzie out the rear window.

4

IT TOOK JOHN a few moments to catch his breath and for the world to stop swirling around him. When he finally got his bearings, he sat up. "Lizzie?" He could barely see the taillights of the car as it disappeared around a bend about a half-mile down the road. John pushed himself up and ran toward a black Jeep Wrangler. He slid behind the wheel and jammed a key into the accelerator. "I'm coming, baby. I'm coming." He backed the Jeep out of its spot and headed off in the direction of the white car.

From their booth, Julia was wondering what was taking John so long when she happened to look out the window just as John sped by in the Jeep.

"Come on," said Julia. "Something's going on."

"We can't just leave without paying."

25

"You pick up the tab and I'll meet you in front with the Buick. But hurry. John just took off in their Jeep and Lizzie wasn't with him. Something's happened and they might need us."

Julia was waiting in the car with the engine running when Paul got in. She hit the gas and headed in the direction she saw John driving.

"Do you even have any idea where we're going?" asked Paul as he buckled his seat belt.

"No," said Julia. "But I do know if I was in trouble, Lizzie would be trying to help me."

Paul just looked at his wife and shook his head.

Lizzie looked out the window and saw nothing but trees with lights from a house now and then set off in the distance. They were on a two-lane back road somewhere north of Lakeside. A tremor of fear began to work its way down her spine from the base of her neck to the top of her buttocks. It was obvious that he wasn't taking her to a police station. But it suddenly occurred to her that the alternative to jail might be worse.

"Where are we going?"

The Stranger drove without talking. They were heading farther away from town, on a country back road. Suddenly, he skidded to a halt, then backed up next to another single-lane road. The Stranger looked around the area for some kind of road markings. He then shrugged and turned down the narrow road. They continued to drive in silence, until they came to a small rise and then on the other side, spread out below in the moonlight was a lake. The Stranger put the car in park and shut off the engine.

Lizzie looked out at the black water. "I'm impressed," said Lizzie. "Not too many people know about Mystery Lake."

"Mystery Lake? Is that what it's called?"

"Well, that's what we call it. I heard that a long time ago, people used to rent cottages on it. But about twenty years ago, the county bought it, closed it off to the public and turned it into a reservoir. That didn't stop some of us from sneaking out here to go skinny-dipping."

He sat in silence staring out at the water, then turned around in his seat holding the gun on her.

"It's changed a lot."

"This place?"

"I was ten when Dad bought the house. It was going to be our summer place. I think it was over there, on the far side. There was a little pier, and a small boat with a little outboard motor. There was a steep road leading down to it and I used to think that our car was going to go into the lake, it was so steep. I spent the whole summer in that house, with my mother mostly. Dad hardly ever made it out because he had to work. My mother refused to spend another summer alone, so she made him sell it."

"Are you gonna kill me?"

The question seemed to startle the Stranger out of his reverie. He looked at the gun and at Lizzie. Something seemed to shift behind his eyes. It was if Lizzie could see his mind at work.

"Here," he said, holding the gun out to her, handle first.

"Is this some kind of trick?"

"Go on. Take it."

She hesitated at first, but then Lizzie reached out and touched the cold steel of the handle, wrapping her fingers around it. She also slid her forefinger through the trigger guard and across the trigger. He was holding the gun by the barrel looking at the finger that covered the trigger. Lizzie started to pull the gun toward her, but he wasn't ready to let go. In fact, he was still gripping the barrel when Lizzie yanked back and the gun exploded.

27

The shot tore through the Stranger's hand and then hit the left side of his forehead. The bullet's impact knocked him back against the steering wheel and then forward between the bucket seats and on top of Lizzie. She looked down at all the blood pouring from the man's head and hand. Blood had also splattered her blouse and the inside of the white car.

"Oh God!" Lizzie screamed. She reached down and shook the man, but he didn't move.

5

OUT ON THE two-lane back road, John was examining the tire marks when he heard the shot.

"Lizzie!" He jumped back in the Jeep and headed down the narrow road in the direction of the gunshot.

"Come on. Wake up," begged Lizzie, but the Stranger just lay there, blood streaming from his head onto Lizzie's lap. "Oh God. What have I done?"

Headlights cut through the trees and reflected off the white car as John pulled up in the Jeep, got out and ran to the Lexus.

"Lizzie! Are you okay?"

He tried to open a door but it was still locked.

"Lizzie, unlock the door."

The door. The remote. She started to hyperventilate and realized she was still holding the gun. A faint wisp of smoke was rising toward the roof of the car.

"Lizzie, the door," pleaded John.

She looked on the floor, and tried to reach under the front seats, but she couldn't find the plastic remote that would unlock the door. Oh no, she thought. She was trapped in here with a dead man, a dead man she had killed. Where was that goddamn thing? She pushed the Stranger's body forward and felt around on the floor and then the back seat. There it was, wedged behind the bottom of the seat and the back. She pulled it out and began hitting buttons until the locks on the doors popped up.

John pulled open the back door. "Jesus Lizzie. What happened?"

"It was an accident. It just went off."

John looked at the Stranger and then around the reservoir. He then looked in the car seat and saw the Stranger bleeding all over the white leather upholstery. "Aw, man. What happened?"

"I'm not sure," said Lizzie. "He was giving me back the gun and it just went off."

"He was giving *you* the gun?"

"I know. It sounds crazy. I didn't mean to shoot him. You gotta believe me."

"Whatever you say, Lizzie."

"It was an accident."

"Sure."

"What's that supposed to mean?"

"I gave you the signal to stop."

"What? You knew this was going to happen?"

"It just didn't feel right," said John.

"He was perfect."

"Well, now he's dead. How perfect is that? Who is he anyway?"

Lizzie opened the glove compartment, reached inside and pulled out a thick yellow envelope. She opened the envelope and looked inside. "John, you're not going to believe this."

John turned toward her and saw her holding the envelope open. Inside was a thick wad of money. She took out the inch-wide stack of money and peeled off a one hundred-dollar bill. She quickly fanned the rest of the bills.

"It's all hundreds and fifties. There's gotta be twenty-five, maybe thirty thousand dollars here."

"Put it back."

"What are you nuts?"

"Just leave it."

"What? So some cop can take it?"

"Who do think carries that much cash around?"

"Who?" asked Lizzie.

John glanced back at the Stranger and was about to turn away when something caught his attention. He looked closer at the man's left hand. He lifted up the man's hand to show Lizzie a diamond and ruby studded gold pinky ring.

"Lizzie, you killed a mobster."

Lizzie looked down at the Stranger. "He doesn't look Italian."

"Not all mobsters are Italian."

"They're not?"

"Was Robert Duvall Italian in *The Godfather*? No. He was Irish. Bugsy Siegel was a Jew."

Lizzie looked closely at the pinky ring. She gave the ring a little tug, but it stopped at the knuckle.

"Lizzie? What are you doing?"

Ignoring her husband, she reached inside her purse, unzipped a compartment, and took out a tube of spermicide contraceptive jelly, removed the top and slathered some on the man's finger. She then twisted and the ring slid off the finger.

"Getting us out of debt, remember?" said Lizzie.

"Shhhh," said John.

"What?"

"I thought I heard a car."

They looked back through the woods and saw the headlights approaching.

"Somebody must have called the police."

"Man, we just can't catch a break," said Lizzie.

But then they saw the Buick pull into the clearing and stop next to the Jeep.

Lizzie stuffed the envelope and ring into her purse. She took a deep breath and stepped out of the white car.

"Julia," she said, running over to her friend.

"How did you find us?" asked John.

"Well, you've got a mean oil leak on that Jeep of yours," said Paul. "You oughta bring it in and let me fix it. We just followed the shiny black spots on the highway."

"Then we saw the headlights from the road," said Julia and figured this was where you were." Julia looked at the Lexus. "Whose is that?"

Lizzie bowed her head and then looked up at Julia. "That belongs to the guy who tried to kidnap me."

"Kidnap! You're kidding?"

"Do I look like I'm kidding?"

"Lizzie, you're bleeding," said Julia, stepping closer to examine the trail of red splotches across Lizzie's chest and shoulders.

"Ah, that's not my blood."

Julia looked up.

"It was an accident, Julia. The gun just went off."

"What?"

Just then Paul turned and looked through the car's window and saw the bloody body of the Stranger in the driver's seat. Paul backed away, then bent over and threw up his chicken and ribs.

Julia looked from Lizzie to the car and then back to Lizzie and John.

"He's in the car?"

Lizzie nodded yes and then opened the front door so Julia could look inside. The Stranger's head was covered with blood, lying motionless.

"Are you sure he's dead?" asked Julia.

"Be my guest," said Lizzie.

Julia leaned inside the car. The first thing she noticed was all the blood, splattered and sprayed in a deKoening design, various shades of red on white leather. The right side of the man's face was covered with a thinning layer of blood that seemed to originate somewhere north of the hairline. Julia took in a deep breath and moved into the car, pushing the man's body over to give her room to sit on the edge of the large bucket seat. She then reached down to the floor where she found a wrist. She pressed the tips of her fingers on the man's veins and waited for some movement, a subtle throb that would indicate a pumping heart and life. Nothing. She noticed his pinky finger was covered with a glistening, gel-like substance. She held it to her nose and breathed. Contraceptive jelly? She lowered his hand, sat back up and looked at the man's neck. It was also covered with blood, but she pressed her finger down on where she thought the large artery should be. Again, nothing. Wiping the blood off her fingers, she backed out of the car and stood up.

"I couldn't find a pulse," said Julia. "We should still get him to a hospital."

"If he's dead, what good is a hospital?" said Lizzie.

"Then we should call the police."

"I don't have a license for the gun."

"So?"

"So if we call the police, I could go to jail."

"You shot a man who tried to kidnap you," said Julia. "It's called self-defense."

"What if they don't believe me? There weren't any witnesses. It's just my word against his and he's dead. Plus, there had to be a dozen people in the bar who saw me dancing with him. You just know somebody's gonna say I lured him out here and then killed him and the charge for that would be premeditated murder. There'd have to be a trial, and even if I'm acquitted people would still treat me as if I was guilty. I need you to be my friend here, Julia."

"Of course. Whatever you need."

Lizzie's eyes filled with tears. "I can't go to jail. I've got a son to take care of. They'll take him away from me."

"You're not going to jail."

"Then you'll help me."

"We'll get you the best lawyer in the country."

"No!" shouted Lizzie. "You're not hearing me. I'm not going to stand trial."

"So what do you want us to do?" asked Julia, feeling torn between wanting to help her friend and the man either dead or dying in the white car.

"Help me push his car into the reservoir."

"You're joking, right?"

"I've never been more serious in my life."

"Lizzie, you're in shock. You're angry."

"I thought you were my friend."

"I am, Lizzie. That's why I can't let you do this."

Lizzie took in a deep breath. She looked at John and then at Julia.

"You're not gonna help me, are you?" said Lizzie.

"Lizzie. You're not thinking right. He was trying to kidnap you. You shot him. No jury's gonna convict you for that."

"I wish I could believe you darling, I really do. But I just don't want to take that chance. Look, the man's dead. I didn't want to kill him, but I did. It was an accident, but I shot him with an unlicensed gun. Now if you could guarantee, and I mean absolutely guarantee, that I would not do jail time for this very suspicious accidental death by an unlicensed firearm, then I'd say okay. But you can't and you know it. So please. I'm begging you, as my best friend, to help me here. Please, Julia. Paul?"

Paul looked at his wife. "I think I'm gonna throw up again." He bent over and lost the rest of whatever was left in his stomach.

"There's got to be a better way," said Julia.

"I'm listening," said Lizzie.

Julia let out a deep sigh.

"Lizzie. I'm sorry about what happened. I really am. But if we don't take that body and turn it into the police and tell them what happened, then we're all going to jail."

"Not if nobody knows but us."

"That's just it," said Julia. "How can you be sure nobody else knows? What if someone was watching from their window or something?"

"You see anybody around here but us?"

"I can't let you do this," said Julia. "I'm sorry."

"No. I'm the sorry one," said Lizzie as she reached in her purse and pulled out the gun and put it to her head.

"Lizzie!" shouted John. "Jesus, what are you doing?"

"Shut up, John. I didn't want to have to do it this way, but you've left me no choice. If I go to jail and they take my boy away, I wouldn't want to live anymore. So if this is the way it has to be, so be it."

Julia felt a combination of rage and helplessness surge through her body. But she couldn't move. Would Lizzie really shoot herself if they refused? At this moment, she wasn't sure. There was a strange look in Lizzie's eyes, as if somehow she had taken a wrong turn down a mental path and it was too late to turn back

"Come on, people," said John. "Don't let us down here. You're the only real friends we have. That bastard tried to kidnap my wife. Paul. You know I'd do this for you if anything like this ever happened to Julia. We're the victims here. Don't let this terrible accident destroy everything we've got. We're supposed to be best friends, and that means when the shit storm comes, we'll be there for each other. Well brother, I believe that storm has arrived."

Lizzie stared at Julia and Julia stared back. She thought she could see something shift behind Lizzie's eyes but she wasn't sure. Then, as if a cloud had lifted, Lizzie slowly lowered the gun and put it in her purse. She then walked to the rear of the white car and put her hands on the trunk. John opened the driver side door and put the car in neutral. He then stood on the side, ready to push. Lizzie looked over at Julia and Paul.

"Aw fuck it," said Paul as he walked over and joined Lizzie at the rear of the car and put his hands on the trunk. They then all looked at Julia.

She felt as if the world was suddenly spinning around her, and that somehow she had become detached from the reality of everyday living. This wasn't happening. This couldn't be happening. Not to her. Not to Julia Ann Stanton of Lakeside, Connecticut, the best oral hygienist in Fairfield County. She just didn't do things like this. It went against every fiber of her body. No matter what this man had done, he deserved better than this. This wasn't right. We can't be doing this.

"It's the only solution," said Lizzie. "I'll die before I go to jail."

Defeated, Julia lowered her head, then looked up at her husband with tears in her eyes.

"On three," said Lizzie, looking directly at Julia. "One. Two. Three."

Lizzie, John and Paul pushed at the same time and for a moment it didn't look as if the heavy car was going to budge. But then it started to roll, crunching gravel under its thick steel-belted tires. Julia kept her eyes locked on Lizzie's as the car moved forward.

The three continued to push as the big car started to pick up speed and eventually careened down the bank on its own. The heavy, white car splashed into the water going about twenty miles an hour, its front end plunging into the gentle waves, leveling out slightly as it gained buoyancy in the water.

Julia watched from the top of the bank. The car looked like a giant white whale as it drifted slowly away from shore.

"It's not sinking," said Paul.

"We should have opened the windows," said John.

Slowly, under its own weight, the car began to sink into the abyss of the black water. They watched silently, until they could no longer see the car beneath the surface. Lizzie walked toward the Jeep. She looked down at the tracks in the gravel, then took some branches and began smoothing out the gravel so it wouldn't look as if a car had been driven into the lake.

Throwing the branch away, she turned toward Julia who just pressed her lips together as tight as she could, afraid that whatever she might say would only make things even worse. Lizzie turned away and walked toward the Jeep.

John walked over to Paul and put out his hand. "Thanks, buddy."

Paul shook his hand and looked at Julia, who just turned away and walked toward the Buick. She got behind the wheel and waited for her husband.

Lizzie started to walk over to her, but John stopped her.

"Come on," he said. "Let's go."

John and Lizzie got in the Jeep and drove off down the narrow road. Julia sat in the Buick and stared out over the lake. Paul opened the passenger door and slid in beside her.

"Un-fucking-believable," said Paul.

Julia lowered her head, too numb to let out the sob that lay heavy at the bottom of her throat. She looked into the rearview mirror to see the taillights of the Jeep fade as it drove off into the night. She watched until the lights became tiny red dots and eventually disappeared.

Julia turned to face the window next to her and stared at the reflection of a stranger. A shudder rippled across Julia's shoulders when she realized that the reflection was hers. She turned on the ignition and backed away from the water, then turned the car around and followed the road through the trees.

6

A THICK FOG had moved inland from the Sound, so it took Julia and Paul longer than usual to drive home. It was nearly one in the morning when Julia finally pulled the Buick into the tar-covered driveway and parked under the carport attached to their white vinyl-sided ranch house. The three-bedroom house was built 37 years ago as part of a sub-division of almost identical homes in a working class section of Lakeside. Typically referred to as a "starter home," which meant its saving grace was that it was supposed to be affordable and temporary, or so Julia and Paul thought when they moved in four years ago. The price was right and it had an enormous bay window in the living room that overlooked a glorious weeping willow tree in the front yard. It was not until several months after they moved in that Julia realized her cherished weeping willow would be a fleeting source of comfort as its winter barrenness lasted far longer than its luscious summer leaves.

Neither had spoken a word since leaving the reservoir thirty minutes earlier. There was a faint smell of vomit surrounding Paul, who looked down to see he still had some residue from his heaving on one of his shoes. Julia turned off the ignition and shut off the headlights. She sat behind the wheel staring ahead, her fingers gripping the steering wheel so tight the palms of her hands were numb.

Paul opened his door and turned toward Julia.

"Honey. You coming in?"

Julia looked out over their third of an acre backyard that ended in an unseen boundary with their neighbor's property. Under the light of the full moon, the backyards looked like they went on forever, long green strips of lawns, swings, and playhouses. It was then that Julia realized her backyard was the only one without a set of swings and her eyes immediately filled with tears. As her vision blurred, her mind filled with images of all the times they tried to conceive, the needle shots of the latest fertility drug in her rear, the temperature taking, how the timing had to be just right.

"Julia?" said Paul.

"Huh?" she answered.

"Are you gonna stay out here all night?"

Julia let go of the steering wheel and rubbed the tears from her eyes.

"You're crying. Oh baby. Don't worry. It's gonna be all right. We just have to put this whole night behind us, that's all."

Julia shook her head, opened her door and slowly climbed out of the car. She took in a deep breath, unlocked the back door, and entered the house through the laundry room, which was attached to the galley-style kitchen and dining area. Julia turned on the lights and leaned against the sink. As soon as Paul entered she looked up. "I'm scared, Paul. I still think we should call the police."

She reached for a wall phone next to the dish cabinet, but Paul put his hand over the receiver before she could lift it.

"Hold on a second. What are you going to say?"

"I don't know. I just know I've got to say something."

"Can we talk about this?"

"What's there to talk about? We helped dump a body into the reservoir."

"It was an accident," said Paul.

"Right, and we're supposed to report accidents. What we did was wrong. I feel sick about it."

"So do I," said Paul. "But what good is calling the police now?"

"I might be able to sleep a lot better knowing I did the right thing."

"See, that's the problem. What's the right thing?"

"Telling the police."

"Not necessarily. That train left the station when we helped push the car into the water. We're accessories, babe. Our prints are all over the car. If we go to the police now, all we're going to do is get into a shitload of trouble. Do you want to go to jail just for helping a friend cover up an accidental death?"

"I don't know," said Julia. "I just can't believe we did this. Oh God!"

"What?"

Julia was looking down at her wrist. "My watch. It's gone."

Julia rushed to the bedroom to check the dresser, the one place where she put it when it wasn't on her wrist. She switched on the light and immediately went to the large Formica dresser, the only piece of furniture in the room that wasn't a hand-me-down. There was some loose change, an extra set of house and car keys, a jewelry box, but no watch. She quickly checked the bathroom sink. "It's not here."

"It'll turn up," said Paul.

"I know I was wearing it tonight," said Julia, rushing back out to the Buick. Paul stayed in the bedroom where he could hear the car door open, and then slam shut a few minutes later. "Jesus," he mumbled to himself, "I'll buy her another watch."

While he waited for Julia to return, Paul sat at the foot of their king size bed, thinking. What really happened at the reservoir? What was Lizzie doing dancing with that guy? She was hiding something. The man was driving an expensive car. That meant he had money. But how much cash would he have had on him? Something else was going on here. Maybe they found a stash of something and they're going to sell it. God knows they need the money. That's got to be it. They found something and they've taken it. That's why they couldn't call the police.

"We have to go back," shouted Julia, almost out of breath.

"What are you talking about? Back where?"

"My watch. It must have come off when I checked the guy's pulse. I think it's still in the car. We have to go get it."

"Are you crazy?"

"You don't understand. It's the watch you gave me for our first wedding anniversary. You had it inscribed. 'To Julia from Paul.' Remember?"

"Julia, it's one o'clock in the fucking morning."

"Here's what we're gonna do," said Julia. "We're gonna go back, get the watch, and wipe down every place we touched. That way there won't be any prints, so when we get home and call the police, we've got nothing to worry about. But we've got to get the watch. You have to figure that if they ever find the body and that watch is there, they're gonna come looking for me, not Lizzie."

"Julia, this is insane. It's the middle of the night. How are you gonna see anything?"

She bolted out the bedroom and into the kitchen where she frantically searched shelf after shelf of their crowded narrow pantry. She pushed aside pancake mix, boxes of herbal tea, hot cocoa mixes, tiny jars and metal boxes of spices and herbs, and stacks of paper napkins. Opened bags of stale potato chips fell on to the floor, along with plastic knives and spoons left over from the Memorial Day barbecue they had had the previous month, but she didn't stop to pick anything up. Suddenly, a wide smile spread across her face as she reached into the back of the cabinet and pulled out an oversized black waterproof flashlight.

"Aw, man," said Paul, "you're really gonna do this?"

"Don't you get it yet? If the police find that watch in the car with the body, they won't even need any fingerprints. They'll just come right over here and haul my ass to jail."

"What are the chances of that?"

"Pretty good I'd say. How many Pauls and Julias do you think there are in Lakeside?"

"Julia, we don't know how deep that car went down," said Paul. "And I ain't that good a swimmer."

"Well I am," said Julia. "Just help me find the snorkel and fins. All you have to do is stand on the shore with a towel for when I come out. I figure the water will be warm enough but it's only about 60 or so outside tonight. Okay? Think you can do that?"

"I guess," said Paul, hesitantly. "But if we see anyone, any cars, or anything, we're outta there. Okay?"

7

MOST OF THE FOG had lifted so the trip back to the reservoir took less than 20 minutes. Another ten minutes were swallowed up as they followed the now dry and harder to see oil spots, searching for the gravel road off Lakeside Drive that led to where the Lexus had been parked. Since Lizzie had raked away the tire tracks they made a few false turns until the headlights picked up something glistening on the edge of the bank and that made them stop.

"There's my puke," said Paul.

Julia put the car in park and got out. She could feel the increased adrenaline rushing through her body as she walked to the edge of the bank. Then she aimed the flashlight into the water where she thought the car had gone in. Meanwhile, Paul opened the trunk and took out a short-handled shovel and began to bury his vomit.

Julia looked out over the stillness of the water. It was as if the body of water had swallowed the man and car whole. Julia hoped the car had not sunk too deeply. She could hold her breath for two minutes, max. She wished she had invested in a diving tank like the one she used when she and Paul went to the Caribbean two winters ago. Not that there'd ever be much use for one, she pondered. How many times in your lifetime would you have to do something like this? Never was the only answer she could think of.

She dipped her hand in the water. Not too cold. It had been warm during the day and the water on the surface at least had retained some of the sun's heat. The night air for June 23rd was a little chillier than normal for this time of year; there was a slight breeze coming from the North. Still, Julia had gone skinny-dipping on nights cooler than this.

She stood up as Paul joined her, carrying a bundle in his arms, which he placed on the bank near the water. Spread out on a thick towel was the facemask, snorkel, and a pair of green fins.

"I knew I'd forget something."

"What?"

"A bathing suit," said Julia as she took off her denim shirt and cowgirl skirt. "What the hell," she added. "It's not like we haven't done this before, right?"

Goosebumps broke out all over her body as she slipped the facemask over her head. She put the snorkel in her mouth and aimed the flashlight toward the water.

"Be careful, baby," said Paul, picking up the towel. "Here, you oughta take this." He handed her an oily rag. "To wipe off the prints."

Julia nodded 'yes' and tied it around her wrist. She then walked to the water's edge, sat down and pulled on the rubber fins. Taking a deep breath, she pushed off into the water.

Holding the light in front of her and aiming down into the water, Julia swam slowly away from shore, searching through the water. She kept her face below the surface, and breathed through the snorkel. The light was a diffused beam beneath the water, picking up reflections from passing fish and plants. She took a deep breath in through her mouth and went beneath the surface, searching for the bottom. She noticed the incline from the bank began to level off about 25 feet under the surface. Where was the car? She looked all around, the beam of light fading off into the distance. She was about to return to the surface for more air when she turned completely around and almost dropped the flashlight. She couldn't gasp because the snorkel filled her mouth and its upper end had sealed itself off when it went beneath the water's surface. A jolt of electricity sent a chill through every cell of her body. There it was, just two feet behind her and back toward the shore. Looking like a giant white sea monster, the car was teetering on the ridge of a sharp drop off, its front two wheels hanging over the edge.

Marking her place in her mind, she raced to the surface to get a mouthful of air. Breaking the water, she gasped in giant gulps, filling her lungs with beautiful fresh life-giving air. She could see Paul waving to her from shore. She was afraid she'd lose her spot so she ignored him and went right back under.

Julia followed the light beam back to the car. This time she reached the rear side door and stopped. She had to be careful here because the slightest movement in the wrong direction could send the car over the edge and down to a depth too far to reach without diving equipment. She reached out slowly and was about to pull up on the lever when the door opened on its own and a two and a half-foot long spotted bass slipped out through the opening. How could this be, wondered Julia. It must have happened when the car hit the water. The back door must not have been closed tightly. Careful not to tip the car, she slowly pulled the door open wider and aimed the flash light inside.

Julia had mentally prepared herself for this moment, to be ready to face the horror she expected to find in the back seat of the car. But she was not prepared for what she saw. She aimed the light beam all around the interior of the car, front and back. It was empty.

"Where is he?" her mind screamed.

He must have fallen out through the open door. Julia quickly searched the area around the car for a body. Nothing. Then she realized she was on the edge of a sharp drop off. She went to the edge and aimed the light down into the blackness. If that's where he was, she wasn't going to find him. It was too deep. She couldn't even see the bottom from the edge. That's what must have happened. She could hear her heart pounding as she returned to the surface for more air. While the top of the snorkel broke through the surface of the water, Julia kept her face submerged and her flashlight aimed at the bottom of the reservoir so she could continue searching for the body. After filling her lungs with air, she returned to the car.

This time she carefully moved into the car and searched the back seat and floor as well as under the front seats, anywhere her watch might have fallen. She felt down behind the seat but pulled her hand away when she felt the car start to tip forward. She backed out of the rear door and searched around the area beneath the car along the ridge. No sign of the watch. Maybe it had fallen out, too. If so, she was never going to find it.

She needed more air so she swam back to the top. She was about to return to shore when she remembered the rag around her wrist. She untied it and swam back to the car to wipe away any trace of their presence. She wiped the rear bumper and trunk area, and the backseat and door where she had been sitting.

After one more search for her watch, Julia was about to return to the surface when the idea hit. She popped out of the water like a seal, gasping for air. She took in another full breath and returned to the car. Swimming around to the rear, she braced herself against the bottom and with one foot, pushed up under the rear bumper. It didn't take much effort to make the car tilt forward and then slowly slide over the edge and disappear into the deep abyss. Dust and debris swirled around Julia as she watched the whiteness of the car fade away. As she swam back to shore, Julia contemplated what she had done and why. Not finding the body had thrown her into a state of confusion. How could she call the police now? What would she tell them? There's a car at the bottom of the reservoir that she helped put there. There had been a body in it, but now it's gone. Sorry.

By the time she climbed out of the water, shivering, the conflicting pulls over what to do had given Julia a migraine headache. Paul quickly wrapped the towel around her and held her tight.

"Jesus, honey, what took you so long?"

"He wasn't there," said Julia between chattering teeth. The night air seemed a lot colder now than when she had first gone in.

"What do you mean?"

"The car. It was empty."

"I don't understand," said Paul staring out at the water.

"The back door was open. He must have slid out."

"But the doors were all closed," said Paul.

"I found one of them open," said Julia.

"What about your watch?"

"Gone."

"No watch. No body. Oh, man."

"I wiped off the prints."

"Good."

"And I did something else."

"What?"

"The car was on a ledge. I pushed it over."

"Good thinking. So you've changed your mind about calling the police."

"I'm not sure," said Julia, pulling on her skirt, and then slipping into her denim shirt.

"Not sure? Baby. We're home free."

"Why? Just because his body wasn't in the car? What if it's lying on the bottom of the reservoir?"

"Yeah? Well maybe that's where your watch is, too."

Julia buttoned her blouse, picked up her boots and walked barefoot to the Buick. She opened the driver side door and got behind the wheel. Paul gathered up the snorkel gear and put it back in the trunk before getting into the passenger side.

"All I'm saying is that maybe we should just wait a couple days."

"Why?"

"Well, first off if there's no body, there can't be a crime, right? What if he isn't even dead?"

"That's even more of a reason to go to the police."

"No. Think about it," said Paul. "Let's say the guy was unconscious the entire time we were there. If he's alive and goes to the police, the only person he's going to turn in is Lizzie, and maybe John if he was somehow involved. But not us, we were just bystanders."

"The word is witnesses."

"Witnesses?" laughed Paul "I believe the correct word is accessories. I sorta helped, remember? That's why you can't go to the police now, even if he is alive."

"I'd just say she forced you. That you didn't have a choice."

"That's not gonna cut it. Okay, she pulled a gun on us and then threatened to kill herself if we didn't help push the car into the water. Here's the problem with you calling the police. It's still our word against Lizzie's. If he's dead and at the bottom of the reservoir and they pull him out, we're gonna be charged with accessories after the fact, or something like that just because how else are we gonna know what happened if we weren't there. Right? Now, if by some miracle he survived, we should just let fate take its course. That's all I'm saying."

"Then maybe I should call Lizzie," said Julia. "Tell her he might be alive."

"Why would you want to do that?"

"Why?" Julia asked, incredulously. "To let her know that maybe she didn't kill somebody. I'd sure as hell want to know."

"Just how do you think 'Dizzie Lizzie's' gonna react when you tell her you went back out to the lake?"

"If I tell her about the watch, she'll understand."

"Let's just think about this, okay? We know something Lizzie doesn't. Maybe he's not dead. Maybe somehow he got out. Personally I think he's fish food. But the main thing is that there's no body in the car. Anyway, here's how I figure it. She pulled a gun on us. I don't know about you but I nearly shit my pants. I say we let *her* sweat it out for a while. You know. Just a couple days. But here's the main thing. They took something off that guy. Money. Drugs. Or whatever. And that's the real reason she didn't want to call the police. Now, you know what really pisses me off?"

"What?"

"That they weren't planning to share any of whatever they got off him with us even after we helped them."

"Whatever it is, I don't want any of it. You should be ashamed of yourself for even thinking like that."

"Okay, how about this? We just teach her a little lesson, that you don't pull this shit on your friends."

"I don't know, Paul. You're starting to sound like her. This can't be about Lizzie. This is about some poor slob whose body might be lying at the bottom of a reservoir

50

because we didn't have the guts to stand up to her. I say we call the police, anonymously if necessary, and tell them we saw something suspicious out by the reservoir. That's all. Let them find the car and a body if there is one. I just don't want to ignore what happened, Paul. What if the guy had a family? Nobody deserves what he got."

"Okay. But not yet. Give it a couple days."

"Why?"

"Just in case, you know, that he made it."

"One day. That's all, and I'm calling it in."

"What about Lizzie? You gonna tell her about going back?"

Before answering, Julia flashed back to some of the nastier things Lizzie had done in the years they had been best friends. One incident that came to mind was the time Julia took another girl's pearl necklace home by mistake after gym class. Somehow the necklace got caught on Julia's spiral binder and she didn't discover it until later that night when she was doing her homework with Lizzie. Julia wanted to call the girl, her name was Brenda something, and tell her she found the necklace. But Lizzie told her not to worry about it. Just give it to her the next day. What was the rush. Julia listened to Lizzie even though she thought it was best to tell Brenda that night. The next day, when Julia returned the necklace to Brenda in school, she noticed some bruises on her face and hands. "What happened?" Julia asked. Brenda's eyes filled with tears as she started to speak. "I wasn't supposed to take my mom's necklace to school. It was an heirloom or something. When I told my father I lost it, he started hitting me. My mother had to pull him away. They were real pearls, you see." Julia remembered the strange look in Lizzie's eyes as she listened to Brenda's tale. It was a look Julia would never forget because it seemed so out of place. Where Julia was feeling nothing but guilt over not calling Brenda the night before, Lizzie seemed to be reveling in the poor girl's misfortune. When Julia confronted Lizzie later that day, the words Lizzie spoke echoed in her mind. "Hey, at least she's got a father. So what if he hits her now and then? I'd take a good spanking any day of the week compared to what I've got, which is nothing. Do you have any idea what nothing feels like? It's ten times worse."

"Where'd you just go?" asked Paul.

"I'm sorry. I was just remembering something Lizzie had said. You're right. She's too unpredictable. I won't say anything to her for a day, but we have to be real careful. If she suspects we're keeping something from her, there's no telling what she might do."

Suddenly, a rustling sound came from a stand of trees near the bank. Paul looked toward the trees and thought he saw movement. "Can we get outta here?"

Julia turned on the ignition as a baby deer and its mother stepped out of the bushes, then ran off into the night. Julia smiled and started to back away from the bank when she hit the brakes. "Wait," she said. "Get out."

"What now?"

"We have to smooth over the tire tracks."

"Oh yeah," said Paul. He climbed out of the car and searched for a branch to use as a rake. As soon as he found one, Julia started backing down the road. Paul followed behind, dragging the branch back and forth across the gravel, smoothing over the tread marks.

When they reached the highway, Paul tossed the branch into the bushes and got back in the car. As soon as his door closed, Julia hit the gas and they drove off as fast as possible without leaving rubber.

Back in the bushes, near where Paul had tossed the branch, there was an impression in the shrubbery that grew along the highway next to the reservoir. It was the kind of impression made by something or someone crawling along the ground. The light from the moon picked up the tiny drops and dampness left on the leaves and stalks that were now bent or broken and pressed to the ground. Some of the drops were darker and thicker than the others; something thicker than water.

8

HE LAY MOTIONLESS until the car was out of sight and the noises of the night returned. The high-pitched thrashing sound of crickets and a million other insects communicating once again filled the forest. For the past hour it had been quiet while the couple in the Buick did whatever it was they had to do. He couldn't see them and they apparently hadn't seen him, which was really all that mattered. Despite the thorns digging into his skin, he had remained as still as death until they left. Now, when he tried to crawl out from under the thick tangle of vines, the sharp curved barbs clawed at his back, arms and legs. Each miniature spike tore away tiny chunks of flesh as he slowly made his way out of the bramble. He kept one arm across his face to protect his eyes. The scratches on his skin would heal quickly, but a scratch on the eye could be far more serious. Finally, he was out of the dense growth and onto the cold surface of the highway pavement.

He tried to stand, but the world began to spin around him so he settled back down and rolled onto his back, staring up at the sky. His wet clothing clung to his body like an extra layer of skin. Fortunately, the night air was too cool for mosquitoes, otherwise he would have been sucked dry by now. There was a constant throb of pain on the left side of his head, and his left hand had no feeling at all. His head wound had stopped bleeding, but the shock of nearly drowning had caused his body temperature to drop and he began to shiver. He knew he had to get medical attention soon or he might die of hypothermia. That's if he wasn't run over first.

He looked down the highway and realized he had no idea where he was. He knew he was near a body of water. In fact, he had emerged from the depths of that body of water about an hour ago. How he got there, however, had been a total mystery until he heard the couple in the Buick talking, and then only some of it started to come back to him in brief but hazy flashes. He could see a woman in a low-cut black blouse smiling up at him. He could see a man jumping on the hood of a car. He could see a gun on the floor of the car. Then an explosion filled his head with bright light and a searing pain shot from his hand to his temple as he fell into a deep sleep. He was in total darkness when he felt water in his nose. He remembered that was what had woken him up. He thought that maybe he was having a nightmare about being trapped in a car at the bottom of a lake. But then he felt the water go up his nostrils and down the back of his throat. The choking sensation brought him back to consciousness. Water was filling the inside of the car and he pushed himself as close to the ceiling as he could to breathe in what little air was left.

When the water rose above his neck and up the side of his face, he took one last breath and let himself fall back to the seat, now under water. He reached for the door and pulled the handle. It wasn't locked, but he had to push hard to open the door because the outside water pressure was higher than inside. But he eventually pushed it open enough to slide out and swim to the surface.

He remembered floating to shore and pulling his bleeding body on to a rocky bank where he lay exhausted, falling in and out of consciousness. But where was all the rest? What else had happened? His memory was like a black hole, an endless void. The sound of a car approaching had awakened him again and he managed to crawl into the prickly bush just as the headlights flooded the bank of the reservoir.

That had been nearly an hour ago. Now they were gone and he was lying in the middle of a country highway, but where? He tried to make sense of the conversation he'd just heard, but the connections between the dots were fading and nothing made any sense. He lay on the highway staring up at the stars when the horror filled him. It was as if someone had lifted up the sticky cellophane and his memory disappeared. It was gone. An image of a computer terminal came to mind. The screen was filled with data, and then suddenly, the screen flickered and the screen went blank. Why had he thought of a computer? As soon as he asked himself the question, the image of a computer faded. Wallet. The answers would be in his wallet. He checked his back pocket where his wallet was supposed to be, but nothing was there.

He then looked at his wounded hand and realized it was closed in a fist. Using his right hand to move the fingers, he pried open the left hand and something fell out onto the pavement next to his head. Searching with his good hand, his fingers found the object and held it up in front of him. It was a woman's gold watch.

As he stared at the watch another image flashed. A soft hand was holding his wrist, then touching his neck. All he could see was her silhouette. She was like an angel leaning over him from another world.

He closed his eyes and gripped the watch. Tell me. Who am I? You can tell me. What happened? How did I get here? What have I done? Out of nowhere, he was filled with a sense of guilt. But what was he guilty of? As soon as he asked himself the question another image flashed. A woman in a pink robe. She's lying on the floor. She's not moving. Her head is turned in an unnatural angle. There's blood on the floor coming from the back of her head. Oh God, he thought. I killed somebody.

Then he felt the vibration coming from the pavement. He put his ear to the road and heard a rumbling sound. Something was coming. Something big. He rolled over on his stomach and began crawling. He looked behind him and saw the lights flickering through the trees, around the bend. He made it off the pavement and onto the dirt and gravel just as the truck was rounding the corner. It was a huge tanker truck and it was slowing down. The driver must have seen him. The large silver tank glistened in the moonlight, which was just bright enough for him to make out the writing on the side of the tank. It said "New England Pool Water." The air brakes hissed as the oversized wheels rolled to a stop. A door opened and then another hydraulic motor came on. The driver was carrying something behind him, sliding it around the tanker. He couldn't see what it was until the driver came around to his side and his mouth dropped open.

"Holy shit," said the driver, holding in his hands a hose with a six-inch opening and screw type nozzle and an oversized wrench under his arm. "What the hell?"

"I've been hurt," the Stranger said. "I need to get to a hospital."

"How'd you git all the way out here?"

"I don't remember," said the Stranger. "Please, can you help me?"

"Aw man. I'm already running three hours late. You're gonna hafta wait till I fill this tank. That's gonna take 30 to 40 minutes."

"Do you have a phone in your truck? Maybe you could call an ambulance."

"Yeah, and maybe I'll just tell the world I'm out here stealing the county's water. Look, pal. I'll give you a ride into town, but you gotta let me fill my tank. That's the best I can do."

"Can you help me into the truck, at least? I don't think I can stand up."

"Lemme git the hose hooked up," said the driver, who when he stepped into the light of the truck cabin, looked a little like Steve Buscemi, a character actor with bulging eyes and a few too many teeth. He gave the Stranger a toothy grin as he wrestled with the long canvas snake, pulling it across the pavement to a brick wall where two hydrants protruded. The driver screwed his hose onto one of the hydrants and then, using the large adjustable wrench, opened a valve that caused the flat hose to rise up and round out as water surged from the reservoir to the tanker truck. That done, he put away his wrench and returned to the Stranger. "You got a mighty bad gash on the side of your head there, mister," he said, kneeling down.

"That's probably why I don't remember anything," said the Stranger. "Maybe you could tell me where we are."

"Well, this here's the Lakeside Reservoir, and this road we're on is Old Lakeside Drive. You really don't remember nothin?"

"Lakeside sounds familiar. Are we in Connecticut?"

"Last I checked," said the driver. "Now, how do you want me to do this? I ain't supposed to do no heavy liftin' cause of my back. Pinched nerve they tell me."

"Just give me something to hold onto. I think I can pull myself up. Then let me use you for support to walk to the truck."

"Okay," said the driver, reaching down under the Stranger to help him up. The Stranger put his arm over the driver's shoulder. "Hey," said the driver. "You're all wet. You're not supposed to be swimming in this reservoir. This is for drinking water."

"And swimming pools, right?" said the Stranger. "It's just water. It'll dry. Help me up."

As soon as he was upright, standing on legs that felt like sponges, the world started spinning out of control, just out of his reach. He had to make it to the truck before he passed out, or the driver would probably just leave him wherever he fell. One step at a time. The passenger door should be getting closer but it looked like it was moving farther away, getting smaller and smaller until he reached out and grabbed the door handle.

The last thing he remembered was feeling the driver's hands pushing him into the passenger seat and then closing the door behind him before he fell back out.

9

WHEN HE REGAINED consciousness, he was lying in a semi-private hospital room. Daylight was streaming through a half-opened window. Looking around, he could see a bed on the other side of the tan curtain was empty. An IV-tube attached to a bag of clear liquid was pumping something into a vein in his left arm. On his wrist he saw a white plastic tag with blue lettering embossed on it. He looked at the name. "John Doe." So they didn't know who he was, either. He then looked at the tips of his fingers and saw the dark smudge marks. They fingerprinted him. Why would they do that?

The body of the woman in the pink robe flashed through his mind again.

The police must have been there. How long had he been out? He checked his wrists for handcuffs. No restraints. Maybe they were waiting for the results of the fingerprints to come back. Next to the bed was a small mirror, attached to a wall mount. He reached for the mirror and pulled it to him so he could see the reflection. Maybe he'd recognize his own face and that would help bring back the rest of his life. But the face that came into view was covered with bandages. All he could see were the eyes and they look frightened.

"Why'd I ever agree to work weekends," muttered Lucinda, a short, attractive Hispanic nurse who wore her stethoscope with the metal end swung over her shoulder like a hunter would carry a rifle. And especially the midnight-to-eight shift. Everybody knew this was the busiest time in the emergency room at Lakeside General, a six-story, 297-bed hospital serving Lakeside as well as Norwalk, Pound Ridge, New Canaan, Darien and other nearby communities. Lakeside General was in fierce competition with Greenwich Hospital, which had the benefit of a teaching affiliation with a medical school. But Lakeside's more diverse population, which included almost fifty percent blacks, Hispanics, as well as first-generation Italians and Russian immigrants, were more comfortable using their local hospital staffed by physicians familiar to them. In fact, some nights, Lucinda could walk down the hallways and hear more languages than she imagined they heard at a general session of the United Nations.

She looked at her watch. An hour to go. She continued on down the hall checking her patients. What a night. Fridays were usually the worst night of the weekend. For many, it meant pay day, which meant money for booze. All that drinking led to more bar fights and domestic squabbles. That was all earlier in the shift. Now, when she looked around the emergency room, she could tell that three quarters of those waiting to be seen didn't look like they had anything resembling an emergency. Nothing more severe than a cold or a cut finger. These were the people who used the ER as an outpatient clinic and their numbers had been growing.

Still, the night had been one long parade of trauma drama. On her shift alone, Lucinda counted two heart attacks, five drug OD's, one diabetic coma, three stabbing victims, and of course the John Doe with a gunshot to the head.

When she returned to the nurse's station, they were still talking about it.

"A truck driver brought him in about four hours ago," said Colleen, the nursing shift supervisor. She was sitting on a swivel stool flirting with a young police officer who must have arrived before Lucinda left for her final rounds.

"As soon as we realized the wounds to the hand and head were caused by a gunshot, we made the call," explained Dr. Rashid to the uniformed policeman, who was writing in a spiral notebook.

"You say he had no identification?" asked the patrolman, whose nameplate said Officer Arden.

"Nothing," replied Lucinda, putting down her clipboard and stepping around behind the counter. "I admitted him. The first things we check are the patient's identification and insurance carrier."

"So you admitted him before finding any of this out," said Office Arden.

"He was unconscious," said Lucinda. "Dr. Rashid approved the admissions because of the seriousness of his injuries. We did make copies of his fingerprints and faxed them over to police headquarters."

"I know. They arrived just as I was leaving," said the officer.

"How come they didn't send a detective?" asked Lucinda. "Usually when we get a shooting victim, they send a detective."

"All the detectives were busy so they sent me to make a preliminary. If we determine he was shot during the commission of a crime, then they'll probably assign a detective to investigate further. What condition is he in?"

"Stable," said Dr. Rashid. "He was a very fortunate fellow. His hand deflected the bullet just enough to prevent it from actually penetrating the skull. In fact, it struck the right exterior temporal bone, but instead of going through, it continued around the outside of the skull, lodging right behind the ear on the other side of the head. The bullet severed several veins, but no arteries, thank God, otherwise, he'd be dead. He might still have some internal injuries from the impact. Even brain damage. We should keep him here for observation."

"Where is he now?" asked Officer Arden.

"Just down the hall. Room 232," said Lucinda.

"Can I talk to him?"

"If he's awake," said Dr. Rashid.

"I checked about ten minutes ago and he was still unconscious," said Lucinda.

"This gunshot wound. Could it have been self-inflicted?" the policeman asked.

"It's possible," replied Dr. Rashid. "But why would he shoot himself through his hand?"

"Right. Let's take a look," said Officer Arden, closing up his notebook.

All three, Lucinda, Dr. Rashid and the patrolman, walked in unison, like the scarecrow, the lion, and the tin man from the Wizard of Oz, down the long corridor. When they reached the entrance to room 232, Lucinda's eyes widened.

"He's gone!" she yelled.

"What?" the doctor asked as he peered into the room. He looked over at the empty bed. Next to it was the IV rig, the metal pole holding the plastic bag with the tube hanging down and dangling in the air. The Patrolman checked the toilet, but found it empty.

"I'll call security," said Lucinda. "He can't get very far."

"What makes you so sure Nurse?" asked the policeman.

"'Cause he's weak and he left his clothes here," said Lucinda, nodding toward a narrow open closet where someone had hung the Stranger's shirt and pants.

The elevator heading for the main floor was filled with doctors in green surgical garb, patients in wheelchairs, and a couple of orderlies with plastic bags of garbage. Standing in the back, dressed in green from head to toe, was the Stranger. He had a green mask and cap on, covering the slightest hint of bandage. No one paid any attention to him. The elevator stopped and everyone stepped off.

At the front desk, an elderly black man wearing a guard's uniform was watching the television monitors when the phone rang. He put the receiver to his ear. "Front desk. Johnson."

"Johnson. Keep on the lookout for a patient. Male. Tall. Over six feet. Possibly still wearing a hospital gown or a robe. If you see him, detain until we get there."

"Yes, sir."

Johnson scanned the area around the main entrance. "I don't see no patients here," he mumbled to himself.

The Stranger saw the guard at the front desk put down his phone and begin looking around the lobby. He immediately did an about face and almost ran into a middle-aged woman in a wheelchair.

"Watch out," said the woman.

"Sorry," said the Stranger.

"Where did that damn orderly go?" said the woman. "I'm supposed to be prepped for a d-and-c in five minutes, and they just leave me here. I don't know what these hospitals are coming to. It's all that HMO crap, isn't it?"

"I'm sorry, ma'am," said the Stranger, his eyes on the guard.

"HMOs. They're ruining the medical profession. Can't get good help any more. Everyone's out to make a buck. I mean, how am I supposed to have surgery if they can't even get me prepped and into pre-op on time?"

"Do you want me to push you?" asked the Stranger.

"Oh Doctor, you don't have to do that. You're all dressed for surgery. You shouldn't be pushing patients around."

"I don't mind," said the Stranger as he got behind the wheelchair and began pushing it down a hallway away from the front desk.

"I'm gonna have to write the hospital a letter about you. I don't believe I've ever received such first class treatment like this. A surgeon escorting me to surgery. I mean, wait till I tell my weight loss group about this."

The woman craned her neck trying to see behind her. "What's your name? I can't quite make out it out."

The Stranger looked down and saw a name stenciled on the surgical gown.

It read: Dr. Wu.

"Here we are," said the Stranger, leaving the woman in her chair outside a doorway. "Someone will be right out."

He started to walk away down the hall.

"Wait! Doctor. I didn't get your name."

The Stranger continued on without turning around.

"What a nice man," said the woman as she turned around and looked up at the door and saw some writing. Squinting at the word, she moved closer until it came into focus. There was just one word painted on the door. "Supplies."

Her mouth dropped open and she looked back down the hallway, but it was empty.

10

JULIA AWOKE with a start. She looked at the alarm clock on the table next to the bed. It was 7:30 in the morning. At least she assumed it was morning. Paul was still asleep, snoring softly into his pillow. The ancient air conditioner was rumbling in the window keeping the room as cold as a tomb, yet she was covered with sweat. Julia wanted to slide back under the comforter and go back to sleep, but as soon as she closed her eyes, the images from the dream filled her mind.

It was a pregnancy dream similar to one she'd had many times before. In this dream, Julia was in a car with another woman. Julia was four months pregnant and not even showing. The other woman was seven months pregnant and very rotund. They were traveling through the countryside of some foreign country when the other woman cried out "It's time. It's coming."

The driver, whose face was in the shadows, pulled the car off the road and Julia climbed into the back seat to help with the delivery. As she held her hand beneath the woman's opening, waiting for the child to emerge, all she could think about was whether the baby was going to be all right since it was being born two months early. A feeling of sadness filled her as she thought about how the baby should have those last two months to get stronger and more prepared for the life that lay ahead. Why was the baby coming early? Was it because the mother just didn't want to be pregnant any more? Julia wrestled with these thoughts as she waited, her hands cupped together to catch the infant's head as it began to crown.

The opening widened as the rounded top of the baby's head pushed through. Suddenly, Julia wondered what would happen if she pushed the head back inside. Give the child some more time in the womb. But then it occurred to her that maybe it was the baby who wanted to come out now. Besides, what right did she have to interfere with the miracle of birth? Just be ready to catch the child as it entered the world. So Julia waited, her hands ready. Only the infant wasn't coming out. Its head was stuck with its tiny nose pressed against the side of the opening. "Please," begged the other woman. "Help me. I can't push any more. You have to reach in and pull him out before he suffocates."

He? How do you know it's a he? Julia asked herself. She looked at the baby's head and saw that it was changing colors. It was turning darker. She had to act quickly. She slid her hand into the woman, feeling the tiny child's back and rear end and tiny arms and legs. Then she felt something else. Something metallic. Her thumb and forefinger pinched together around the object while she used her palm to press against the baby's slippery bottom. Then, holding onto the object and pushing against the child, she pulled her hand forward. The woman cried out. "Faster! Faster!"

Slowly, the newborn came out, covered with blood and embryonic fluid. It seemed to take forever, as if the child's body had elongated as it emerged. But then Julia realized that what she was seeing was the snake-like umbilical cord that was attached to the baby's belly and still connected to the placenta inside the mother's womb. "My baby. Let me have my baby," cried the woman. Julia handed the infant to his mother. As she felt the child being taken from her, she looked down at her hands. There, still pinched between her thumb and forefinger, was a gold watch covered with blood and afterbirth. She wiped it off on her blouse, leaving a red smear. She turned it over and saw the familiar inscription. "To Julia from Paul. I love you."

She was staring at the inscription when the driver turned around in the front seat of the car and reached out toward Julia. "I'll take that," he said. Julia looked up and dropped the watch when she saw his face. It was the Stranger and he had a bullet hole in his left temple.

"No!" she screamed and reached for the door handle, but the door was locked. She was pulling on the handle when she woke up.

What have we done? Julia asked herself. She climbed out of bed and ran to the bathroom, holding a hand over her mouth. She bent over the toilet just in time as her stomach involuntarily heaved its contents into the porcelain bowl. Using toilet paper to wipe her mouth, she flushed the toilet and then turned on the shower. She waited for the water to cool then stepped beneath the pounding spray, letting the hard pulsing streams jab her skin like a thousand needles. What they did was wrong and she felt ashamed of herself. She turned the lever on the shower toward hot. The water burned into her skin, turning it a bright pink. "Oh God!

Please forgive us," she cried as she pushed the lever further to the left. The water got even hotter as the shower filled with steam. She let go of the lever and slid down the tile siding until she curled into a ball at the bottom, letting the scalding shower sear her back until it turned red where the water burned into her.

"What the hell are you doing, Julia?" shouted Paul as he reached in and turned off the water. "Jesus Christ, I burned my hand."

Paul reached down to his wife as she curled into the corner of the shower stall. She was crying and shaking as he kneeled down next to her. Finally, she looked up at him with a deep sadness in her eyes that he had never seen before.

"Aw, baby," said Paul, putting his arm around her shivering shoulders. "Don't be doing this. Goddamn that bitch! Lizzie's gonna pay for this. I don't care if she is your best friend. She's evil. I just knew something like this was gonna happen. I don't know how John puts up with her. I woulda kicked her ass out the door a long time ago."

"Paul, would you get me a towel."

"Sure honey," he said, reaching up and pulling a thick bath towel down off a shelf next to the sink. He wrapped it around her and held her to him. "I'm gonna take care of you, baby. You don't worry about nothing, okay?"

Julia closed her eyes and called up the image of Lizzie, holding the gun to her head ready to kill herself. As hard as she tried, Julia could not feel anger toward her friend. Instead she felt sorry that Lizzie felt compelled to do what she did in order to survive. She knew Paul would never understand. For some reason, Paul had long ago accepted his lot in life and had given up on his dreams. But she and Lizzie shared a bond. It was a bond similar to one shared by prisoners, or soldiers trapped in battles they were forced to fight.

Julia thought about how she'd always looked up to Lizzie, how she admired her friend's brazenness and fearlessness, especially when they were in high school. She recalled the night a group of girls from a tough crowd tried to bully Julia at a school dance. Lizzie stood next to her and just smiled at the lead bully as if she was going to enjoy whatever was about to happen. The leader backed down and left them alone for the rest of the night.

She opened her eyes and looked up at her husband who was still holding her from behind. She could feel him becoming aroused as he pressed against the towel wrapped around her waist and chest. It reminded her of why she married a man who would never amount to much professionally or financially. While Paul may be lacking in ambition, he was a consistently satisfying lover. It was the main reason Julia accepted his proposal despite protests from her parents that he would never amount to anything and that she could do a lot better. She had just graduated from oral hygienist school and was about to begin sending out job applications when she met Paul. He was playing pool with a group of friends and he looked like a young Robert Redford. She was with Lizzie at the bar and Lizzie said. "If you don't go over there and cut that boy loose from the herd then I'm gonna have to do it. And you know when I get through he ain't gonna be much good to you, is he?"

Julia drank down a vodka martini for courage and approached the handsome young man in his gas station uniform. He made a corner shot and straightened up as she walked across the room. Their eyes met and from that point on, they were together.

Julia had been saving money to take a trip to Europe, but after her fourth date with Paul, he asked her to marry him and she said yes.

While she had been with a few boys since high school, Paul had been the first man to bring her to orgasm. She even felt a little ashamed for making good sex her number one priority in choosing a mate, especially when all the new women's magazines encouraged their readers to strive for deeper, emotional and intellectual compatibility. Julia knew in her heart that good sex was not enough to sustain a marriage, but it sure helped. Especially in times like these, when the rest of their world seemed to be coming apart.

So she turned around to face him, letting her towel fall to the floor. A boyish grin spread across his face as she reached out and pressed her hand against him.

Without speaking, Julia led her husband back to their bed and for the next hour let her worries and fears wash from her mind as another, deeper primordial passion exploded on the shoreline of her consciousness.

11

THREE MILES AWAY, on the south side of Lakeside, Lizzie lay in her bed staring at misshapen stains in the ceiling, listening to the silence. She could almost hear the paint cracking and peeling on the outside of her three-bedroom split-level house, which was in need of more than just an exterior paint job. The upstairs bathroom was leaking somewhere behind a wall on the lower level, where the wood siding was beginning to warp. Shelves were falling down in the pantry and one of the gutters had pulled way from a drain under the roof and water was now running down the side of the house, causing the shingles in its path to rot away. What was John waiting for, the entire house to collapse? As a carpenter, he was like the barber who always needed a haircut, or the dentist with bad teeth. He'd spend hours repairing other people's homes, but could he lift a hammer to help his own home?

Lizzie had been up most of the night, tossing and turning, replaying the incident of the night before, living out all of her options, all the things they could have done differently. Each choice seemed better than the one they had made. The one that cost a man his life and possibly her friendship with the only person in the world she gave a damn about.

Eventually, she slept for an hour, waking up before sunrise. For the past two hours, she lay in bed staring at the ceiling, searching for ways to make it up to Julia. She never should have forced her to help. That was stupid and cruel. Still, there's no way to re-do the past, no take-two like in some movie being made. Julia would just have to get over it, and Lizzie would just have to do something to win her back. Julia was the only one who came close to understanding why Lizzie behaved the way she did. All her life, Lizzie felt like she was the female equivalent of Holden Caulfield, the boy from *The Catcher in the Rye*, always misunderstood and misbranded, always categorized as a problem child with delinquent tendencies.

Lizzie slid out of bed, walked into the living room and to the front door. She opened the door and looked outside, half expecting to see the Lakeside Police force parked in front, their guns drawn, and someone with a megaphone telling her to come out with her hands up. Instead, she saw her front yard, the tall grass needing to be mowed and Brian's bicycle lying across the walkway where it could trip the most people.

The morning paper was in its plastic wrapper in the driveway next to the Jeep. Lizzie put on her housecoat and walked outside to get the paper. Walking back, she quickly scanned it for any stories about a body found in the reservoir, but there was nothing. She left the paper on the kitchen table and let out a deep sigh. A wave of fatigue rolled over her like the ghost of insomnia.

She returned to the bedroom where morning sunlight was spraying through the white plastic window shades. If Brian had been home, he'd already be in her bed jumping up and down begging someone to bond with him. Still tired from not being able to sleep, she climbed back into bed. It was eight a.m. and John was still asleep. She moved under a flowered comforter and closed her eyes, hoping to slide back into slumber. Instead, visions and thoughts sprayed across her mind. She saw the Stranger holding the gun out to her, and then the gun went off. Lizzie sat up and looked over at her husband. He was snoring lightly. She wanted to wake him, but what good would that do? She knew her marriage had been over for years, and that she just didn't want to deal with it. She kept thinking about Brian and what a divorce would do to him. She'd already seen what it did to his friends whose parents had split up. How depressed they were whenever they slept over. How they'd wake up crying in the night for one parent or the other. So she kept up the façade. She used to tell herself that at least John was a good provider, but lately, even that wasn't true. Now, all he did was take up space and create more dirty laundry.

Lying there, she began to feel horny. She looked over at John, snoring lightly. Might as well let him sleep for all the good he'd be in times like these. She needed a quick fantasy lover. She closed her eyes and saw the image of the Stranger, leaning against the bar in the Ostrich. Lizzie put her hands under the covers and started to massage herself, replaying in her mind another scenario. She imagined that she and the Stranger were in the back seat of his car and he was licking her breasts. Slowly, he moved down her stomach and between her legs. His tongue thrust deep into her opening, flicking her clitoris like a hummingbird until she shuddered in orgasm. The vibration of the bed almost woke John, but he merely shifted on his side and continued sleeping.

She reached out and stroked the side of his face and ran her finger along the lines that had formed around his eyes. Poor John, she thought. It must be killing him inside. Not being able to perform. She knew that for some men, impotence meant death. She wondered if her husband ever thought about killing himself. If she was a man and couldn't have sex any more, she pondered if she would consider death a conceivable alternative. Especially if she'd been as sexually active as John had been.

They had sex the night they met. Lizzie had been a topless dancer at the Jaguar Club in Norwalk when she and the other girls were hired for a special benefit performance at the Lakeside Country Club. It wasn't a dance job exactly. They were hired to be caddies. Topless caddies. And golfers paid an extra hundred dollars to have their clubs handed to them by a topless dancer. John was with the group who drew Lizzie for a caddy and he promised her an extra hundred if she helped him with his putter later on. Lizzie didn't consider what she was doing prostitution because she really liked John and would have done it for nothing. The one thing she never counted on was getting pregnant, but John did the right thing and married her as soon as she told him.

Meanwhile, the country club raised over $12,000 for a local charity, but drew the ire of local church and civic groups who threatened to boycott the golf course over the stunt. The public relations nightmare continued when the *Lakeside Times* reported that a busload of fifth graders had seen a few of the bare breasted ladies near the 14th hole. The club promised to never do such a fool thing again.

Lizzie was staring at her husband when the front doorbell chimed. She looked at the bedroom clock. It wasn't even eight o'clock yet. Couldn't her grandmother sleep in at least once in her life? Lizzie crawled out of bed and went to the front door.

The bell chimed again as Lizzie opened the front door. "Well, look who the cat dragged home," she said, smiling down on her five-year-old son."

"Hi Mom," said Brian. He dashed past his mother as soon as the door opened, bolted for the family room, and turned on the television.

"So I'm the cat now," said Rebecca Davis, who was 78 but looked a lot younger.

"It's just an expression, Grandma," said Lizzie. "How'd it go?"

"He was fine, as usual. You gonna invite me in?"

"Oh, I'm sorry. Come on in. You want some coffee?"

Mrs. Davis looked at Lizzie, who had let her housecoat come open, revealing a see-through nightgown that did little to hide her body.

"Cover yourself up, girl," said Mrs. Davis stepping into the house. "You don't want your son to see you like that."

Feeling the anger flush her cheeks, Lizzie pulled her housecoat together and tied the belt in front. "That better, Grandma?"

"I shouldn't have to tell you," said the older woman, who was wearing a sleeveless, tight-fitting tennis outfit. She followed Lizzie into the kitchen. "I can't really stay long. I've got a set of doubles at nine."

Lizzie ground some coffee beans and put them into a mesh funnel, then poured ten cups of water into the rear of the drip grind coffee maker.

"Grandma. I need a real big favor."

"What is it this time?" Mrs. Davis asked, sitting down at the kitchen table. She started reading the paper while Lizzie got down two cups.

"I might need you to take Brian for a while."

"What's a 'while' and why?"

"John and me. We're going through a bad patch here. We just need some time to work things out."

"He needs to go to work is what he needs," said Mrs. Davis. "I see what's going on here. You working day and night and he sits on his ass all day drinking beer and watching TV."

"He tries," said Lizzie. "It's just things are slow right now in the home construction business."

"What? He can't do something else? Look-it here." She opened the paper to the help wanted section. "Five full pages of jobs. You gonna tell me there ain't something here he could do?"

"He's a carpenter, Grandma."

"He can count, can't he? Add, subtract. Here's a job right here at Grade Supermarket. Jesus, with all them computers doing all the figuring for you, you don't even have to know how to count."

"I'll tell him about the job. But it's more than that. We need some time alone. It'd just be for a few days. A week at the most."

"I don't like it. The boy needs to be with his mother and father. Besides, I play tennis two to three times a week. What am I gonna do with him then?"

"He can watch. Please, Grandma. We could use the time to help find John a job."

"Well, at least you ain't asking for more money. I can't believe how you two pissed away every penny I ever gave you and then some. Other people get by, why can't you?

"We're okay for now."

"It's about time. You just ain't never learned to save is all. You get it and spend it. Then you borrow more and spend it. And them credit cards. Jesus, how much you owe now?

"Grandma. We don't need your money. We just need you to look after Brian."

"I'll tell you what," said Mrs. Davis, standing up. "If John gets a job, then we'll see."

"You don't want your coffee?"

"I don't like to drink too much coffee before a tennis match." She looked through the door to the family room and saw Brian glued to the television set. "Like father, like son."

"I'll call you," said Lizzie walking Mrs. Davis to the door.

"So what did you do? Win the lottery?"

"What are you talking about?"

"Lizzie darling. This is the first time I ever left your house without you asking for a little tied-me-over money."

"Ah, I helped one of the neighbors sell their house. They gave me a commission, that's all."

"So now you're selling real estate without a license."

"Grandma, it was just a neighbor."

"You forget, young lady, that I'm the one who raised you. So don't try to pull your stunts with me. I know all too well how that devious mind of yours works. And someday it's gonna get you into big trouble."

"Thanks for being so understanding."

"Don't get snotty with me. Now you get in there and start paying some attention to that boy of yours before it's too late."

"Don't start preaching to me about how to be a parent seeing you did such a great job with my mother."

"Unfortunately, I see a little too much of your mother in you. God help us all."

With that, Mrs. Davis turned and walked to the street and got into her car.

Lizzie watched from the door as her grandmother drove away. When Lizzie stepped back inside and closed the front door, there were tears in her eyes. She quickly wiped them away before anyone could see them. It was one lesson her mother had branded into Lizzie as a child. Never let them see you crying. It's a sign of weakness, and it makes them think it's okay to attack you. Another thing her mother taught her was to never let your guard down and to never, ever trust anybody, especially family members, because they're the ones who'll break your heart and betray you when you need them the most.

When Lizzie returned to the kitchen, John was waiting there, pouring himself a cup of coffee. "Your grandmother don't like me much, does she?"

"It's nothing that a little effort toward employment won't cure."

"We gotta talk about last night," said John, glancing at the papers open to the help wanted section. He looked at them and shoved the paper across the table.

"What about last night?" said Lizzie, pouring herself a cup.

"What do we do if the police find the car?"

"We don't do anything."

"What about fingerprints?"

"I ain't never been fingerprinted. Have you?"

"When I worked for that government contractor they fingerprinted me.

"Yeah, but would the police have them?"

"Jesus, I don't know," said John, putting his coffee down. "Why'd ya hafta shoot him?"

"I told you, it was an accident."

"We fucked up."

"Yeah. Well. It's too late to do anything about it now."

"Maybe we could still go to the police. Tell 'em how you was kidnapped and how you had to kill him to protect yourself."

"And how are we gonna explain why we pushed his car in the lake?"

Before John could respond, he looked over at the doorway and saw Brian standing there. Brian walked over to Lizzie and stood in front of her. "I had a nightmare at Grandma's."

"You did. What happened?"

"A monster tried to kill me. A big monster. With one eye."

"Ooo," said John, joining in. "How'd you get away?"

"I woke up."

"Good boy," said Lizzie, taking her son up on her lap. "Always remember, that whenever the nightmare gets too scary, just wake up and everything will be all right." She was looking at John when she said it.

12

THE STRANGER sat in a booth by the window watching the hospital entrance across the street. He had found $4.57 in a pocket of Dr. Wu's surgical gown and had used all but fifty cents of it to buy coffee and a ham and cheese omelet in the restaurant directly across the street from the hospital. The place obviously catered to the hospital staff because no one gave his medical attire a second look.

While sitting in the booth, he had seen two more Lakeside police cars and a plain-looking sedan that appeared to be an unmarked police car arrive at the hospital. It wouldn't be long before they extended their search to outside the hospital, and possibly even the restaurant where he sat.

Part of him wanted to give it up. Just walk across the street and surrender. At least he'd be able to find out who he was. But the arrival of the unmarked car bothered him. That usually meant detectives. What if he was a wanted man who had committed a serious crime? What good would finding out who he was be if it meant spending the rest of his life in jail?

Now that he had eaten, what he desired more than anything was to find some place safe to sleep. But where, and how could he pay for it? What about a park bench? Would he be safe there? Where do homeless people go in Fairfield County, Connecticut? He had to get inside somewhere. The police would certainly be checking the parks, the bus station, even hotels.

As he pondered his dilemma, he saw two policemen step out of the front entrance of the hospital. They talked for a minute, then one started walking down the street, looking into cars, while the second one began to cross the street heading directly for the restaurant.

"You want some more coffee, Doc?" asked a heavy-set man with a dirty apron around his waist.

"No thanks," said the Stranger, standing up.

"You don't look so good. You sure I can't get you something else?"

The Stranger turned and saw the policeman was about twenty yards from the door. "I just need to use your restroom."

"Right back there, second door on the right."

"Thanks." The Stranger walked quickly toward the restroom keeping his back to the front door. He could even hear it open just as he arrived at the men's room. But then he saw another door with a sign that read "No Admittance." He turned the handle, the door opened outward, and the Stranger stepped through. He found himself in a narrow hallway that led to another door. He walked down the hall and opened the second door. This time he found himself outside, on a porch behind the restaurant. There was an open, overgrown lot and wooden stairs leading up to a second landing. Behind him, he heard a male voice say, "You sure he went to the men's room?"

He heard another door open, so he quickly ran up the stairs to the second floor of the porch. There he found a natty looking pale green sofa, with its arms worn thin and one of the pillows stained with a large bluish blotch. He lowered himself down behind the sofa and curled into a ball, hoping his green surgical garb would blend in with the sofa. He could hear the sound of footsteps on the porch below.

"He ain't out here. What's up there?"

"That's where I live," said the voice of the man who asked if he wanted more coffee. "This is my place."

"You mind if we have a look?"

"Lemme get a key. I keep it locked up while I'm down here."

The Stranger heard the sound of a door open and close and then footsteps on the stairs. He squeezed in tight next to the far end of the sofa and prayed that he was invisible. Footsteps scratched across the floor of the porch and someone jiggled the door handle.

"It's still locked," said a male voice. "No windows broken. Doesn't look like he went inside." Another voice called up from below. "You want me to forget the keys?"

"Yeah. I'm coming down." The footsteps left the porch and began to descend the wooden stairs. The Stranger remained in his balled position until the footsteps reached the bottom floor. He then looked out and saw that he was alone.

"He must have run off across the lot," he heard the owner say. "That alley over there comes out on Broad Street."

He tried to pull himself up but when he did, the world started to spin again. He settled back down and closed his eyes. Whatever painkiller he'd been given in the hospital was wearing off and a slow moving ache was forming inside his left temple and spreading like a snake around his skull, over his ear, around the back and to the other side.

He opened his eyes but everything seemed out of focus. He looked at the railing that ran around the outside of the porch. It came into sharp focus and then became blurry. This happened with everything he looked at and it was making him nauseous. Bile filled his throat and he could feel his omelet begin to reverse its digestive direction. The pain in his head suddenly exploded and a cold chill shuddered across his shoulders. He wanted to scream, to call out for help. His mouth was open as wide as it could go but no words came out. The pain in his head became so overwhelming he began to think that death would be a welcome alternative. Anything to make it go away.

He closed his eyes again and an image flashed. It was a little girl. A pretty little girl in a white dress. She was waving goodbye. Another image crashed through. It was the woman in the pink bathrobe and she was saying something to him but he couldn't hear her voice. Then everything turned red as the pain behind his eyes intensified. He had to find something for the pain. Holding on to the back of the sofa, he moved slowly toward the door the policeman had tried to open. He turned the handle. It was still locked. He searched around the molding above the door for a key but all he found was dirt. He looked under the welcome mat but there was nothing there either. On the far side of the porch was a window, but he could see it was locked. He took off the surgical gown and wrapped it around his good hand, then punched out the glass in the window. He reached inside and unlocked the latch, then opened the window and climbed through it.

He found himself standing in a bedroom, next to an unmade bed and pile of dirty clothes. There was a dresser, with a drawer opened and underwear sticking out. He quickly left the bedroom and found the bathroom, which contained a toilet and shower, but no bathtub. There was a thin coating of black grunge on the floor of the shower and the sink looked like it had never been cleaned. Over the sink was a yellowing mirror and medicine cabinet, which he pulled open. Scanning the rusty shelves, he found some hemorrhoid cream, deodorant spray, antacid tablets, eye drops, ear wax remover, and four different brands of pain relievers. He took two of each, plus a few more for later and then left the bathroom.

He had to think so he sat down in an overstuffed chair in what passed for a living room, although it was the only room in the apartment that didn't looked lived in. The chair was not as comfortable as it looked, but it offered enough relief to allow the painkillers to begin their mission.

His memory of anything prior to waking up in a car at the bottom of a lake was still a blank slate. Maybe if he took it back slowly. How did he get in the car? Whose car was it? He was in the back seat, so it probably wasn't his car, or was it? What kind of car was it? He couldn't remember. It was white, though. With lots of leather. That was it. He then remembered one more thing. He reached in the pocket of the green surgical pants and pulled out the watch.

He held it up to his eyes and studied it. Whose watch was this? Why did he have it? He then turned it over to read the engraving again. "To Julia from Paul. I love you."

Was his name Paul? Was Julia his wife? Was Julia the woman in the pink robe?

A wave of exhaustion swept over his face, causing his eyes to close. With it came a thought. If I sleep, maybe I'll dream. And if I dream, maybe I'll remember who I am.

He could feel himself fall into a deep, black hole. It was a slow fall, like a skydiver in slow motion. If he hit,

would he die? Would the parachute open? Did he even care
anymore?

13

PAUL WAS SITTING at the kitchen table in his underwear, eating Cracklin' Oat Bran in one percent milk when Julia came in wearing her white dental hygienist's uniform.

"You're really going to the office?"

"I told you. Dr. Jacobs scheduled a root canal this morning for Mrs. Pershing. She called in yesterday claiming it was an emergency," Julia explained as she poured herself a cup of black coffee. "I should be back before lunch."

"Maybe I'll go over to the garage then," said Paul. "Pick up a little overtime."

"Can't you just wait here? I'm only gonna be gone a couple hours at the most."

"Why? Are you afraid I might say something?"

"No. I just thought it would be best if we were together today."

"How are we gonna be together if you're at the dentist office?"

"Forget it," sighed Julia as she walked toward the door.

"You don't trust me."

Julia was about to leave when she stopped and turned toward her husband.

"I want you to promise me something."

"What?"

"That you won't do anything stupid."

"What is it you think I'm gonna do?"

"Just leave her alone."

"Who?"

"You know what I'm talking about."

"What's wrong with taking advantage of an opportunity?"

"Don't do it."

"I'm not afraid of her."

"That's your first mistake."

"After what she put us through, I think..."

"Stop thinking, Paul. I'll be back in two hours and we can talk about it then, okay?"

"If I'm not here, I'll be at the garage."

Julia shook her head and walked out the door. Driving to the dental office, she kept replaying what Paul had said, that John and Lizzie may have found something valuable in the car. It was definitely a possibility. Especially after what Lizzie had told her about their debt situation. Would Paul be dumb enough to try to blackmail them into sharing whatever it was they took? Unfortunately, the answer Julia came up with was yes. She would just have to talk him out

89

of it. That would really push Lizzie over the edge, if she wasn't there already.

Maybe she should have called Dr. Jacobs and told him she wouldn't be able to assist this morning, that he'd just have to get somebody else. But she was the one who volunteered for the job because it gave her another chance to participate in some real dentistry. She'd been taking courses at night to fulfill the requirements she still needed for dental school. She was about eight credits shy of being able to apply. One day, she would be manning the high-speed drill with the dexterity of a master sculptor, but for now, just taking part in the process was better than scraping tartar all day. It would only take two hours. How much trouble could Paul get into in two hours? She decided not to think about that.

When Julia arrived at the office, Dr. Jacobs' car was already there, alongside another vehicle that probably belonged to Mrs. Pershing. Julia parked the Buick and dashed inside.

A woman in her 60s was sitting in the dental chair with a grimace of pain on her face when Julia entered the small, cramped office.

"Good morning Mrs. Pershing," said Julia, smiling at Dr. Jacobs. "Sorry I'm late."

"Actually, you're on time," said Dr. Jacobs, a thin, balding man in his late 40s. "I was here early catching up on some journal reading when Mrs. Pershing showed up about five minutes ago, so we're just getting started."

"Is this gonna hurt?" asked Mrs. Pershing. "I heard it really hurts."

"Not the way we do it, right, Julia?"

"That's right, doctor."

"Would you prepare a swab and the novocaine?"

Julia opened a small jar and dipped a cotton swab into the external numbing compound. She handed it to Dr.

Jacobs, who dabbed the inside of Mrs. Pershing's cheek and gums.

"You might feel this a little," said Dr. Jacobs, nodding toward the needle wrapped in cellophane. Julia removed the outer cover, and plunged the tip into an amber jar containing a clear liquid. She filled the needle and was about to hand it to Dr. Jacobs when she stopped.

"What's the matter?" asked Dr. Jacobs.

"I was just thinking," she said. "If we were in a hospital, and I was a nurse, this would be my job."

Mrs. Pershing looked over at Julia with a concerned look on her face.

"What are you talking about?"

Mrs. Pershing turned toward Dr. Jacobs, a pleading in her eyes.

"Giving her the needle. The novocaine. I can do this."

Mrs. Pershing looked back at Julia, her eyes widening.

"I'm sure you could, Julia. But the State of Connecticut could also revoke my license if I let you."

The woman now turned toward Dr. Jacob, gripping the side of the chair. She looked like she was ready to bolt.

"It's not fair. Nurses give shots all the time."

"But this isn't just giving a shot. This is administering an anesthetic."

"Oh dear," blurted Mrs. Pershing."

"I could still do it," said Julia. "I've been practicing on oranges."

"Maybe this isn't a good time," said the elderly woman.

"It's against the law. Now give me the needle," demanded Dr. Jacobs.

"It's a dumb law," said Julia, handing Dr. Jacobs the needle.

"Open wide, Mrs. Pershing," said the Doctor, pulling his face-mask over his nose.

Mrs. Pershing glanced up as Dr. Jacobs held the needle to the light to check the amount of novocaine he was about to administer. He was about to plunge the needle into her gums when she grabbed his arm.

"I can't do this."

"Whatta ya mean? It's gonna be fine."

"Can't you knock me out with gas or something?"

"We don't use gas any more. Besides, this is better. It's just novocaine." Dr. Jacobs glaring at Julia. "Let's be a big girl, now. That's right. Open wide."

Julia looked down at the woman and smiled, hoping to soothe some of the fear in her eyes. She then noticed something through the window that gave her a chill. While Dr. Jacobs administered the novocaine, Julia looked outside and saw Lizzie's Jeep driving by with Lizzie behind the wheel talking to someone on a cellular phone. Suddenly, Julia felt frozen with fear.

"John, listen to me," shouted Lizzie into the small flip phone. "Hold on a second. Let me close the window so I can hear better." She set the phone down on the passenger bucket seat and pushed a silver nub that closed her driver's side window, silencing the sounds of the street whooshing by. Still holding the steering wheel with one hand, she picked up the phone and continued her conversation. "John, will you shut up and just listen to me."

She looked at her watch as she pulled to a stop at a red light.

"I didn't have time to discuss it. I'm sorry. But this guy eats breakfast at the diner every Saturday morning between ten and ten-thirty."

"Don't you think you're taking an unnecessary risk here?" said John.

"I'm just gonna have him look at the ring."

"You really want to get us killed, don't ya?"

"Nobody's gonna get killed."

"Oh, yeah? Tell that to the poor schmuck in the reservoir."

Lizzie looked at the phone and rolled her eyes. "I'm on a cell phone, asshole. Watch what you say."

The light changed to green and Lizzie continued driving. "How's Brian doing?"

"He's fine. We're watching wrestling."

"I'll just work one shift. If Lou wants me to stay on past six, he can shove it."

"Just be careful with this guy, okay?"

"I'm always careful, baby."

"I still think it's risky. How much could it be worth?"

"We'll know soon enough. Gotta go. I'm here." Lizzie punched the end button and closed up the phone as she pulled into the Lakeside Diner.

She turned off the ignition and looked at her watch. Ten after ten. She saw Eddie the Hand's black Camero at the far end of the parking lot. She took another look at the ring. It was solid gold inlaid with several large diamonds. She figured the diamonds alone should be worth several thousand dollars.

She slipped the ring in a pocket of her light blue waitress outfit and walked through the front door of the diner.

14

WHILE THE YEARS since high school had been
financially kind to Eddie the Hand, he had let himself go in
the physical fitness department. As she approached his
table, Lizzie estimated he had put on at least 100 extra
pounds since he sat behind her in homeroom. He was
sitting alone in a booth in the smoking section. Eddie was
eating a plate of corned beef hash with two eggs over easy
and plenty of catsup. He was dipping a piece of toast into
the broken yolk on top of the hash when Lizzie took the
empty booth across from where he was sitting.

"Hey Eddie," she said, sliding into the booth.

"Lizzie baby. How about some more coffee?"

"In a minute, Eddie. I wanta show you something."

Eddie looked up from his meal and wiped his mouth with his napkin. He was wearing a blue blazer, chinos and white shirt and looked like he just stepped off a yacht. He ran a hand back over his mousse-slick black hair and took out a cigarette. Lighting it up, he saw Lizzie staring at the pack so he held it out to her and she took one. After lighting it for her, he sat back and smiled.

"So. What's this thing you wanta show me?"

"This," she said, reaching into her uniform and pulling out the ring. She placed it on the table next to his hash and eggs.

He picked up the ring and held it in the palm of his hand. "Heavy. Solid gold?"

"I think so," said Lizzie.

He then reached into his jacket and took out a black metallic tool with a sharp pointed end. Working the tool into a notch on the ring, he levered out one of the diamonds. He then took out a pair of tweezers and held the diamond up to the light.

Turning the diamond in the light slowly, he counted to himself and nodded.

"Where'd you get the ring?"

"I, ah, inherited it."

Eddie took a drag on his cigarette and just stared at her.

"From an uncle on my mother's side," she added. "It's been in the family for years."

"Sure it has." Eddie took another drag then snubbed out the smoke. He took out a jeweler's magnifying glass and studied the rest of the diamonds in the ring. He rolled the ring around under the glass and smiled. He then put the jeweler's glass away along with the rest of his tools. He pushed the diamond he had removed back into its place and handed the ring to Lizzie.

"So, what's it worth?" asked Lizzie

"That depends."

"On what?"

"Lots of things."

"You mean like sentimental things. It is kind of a family heirloom."

"Heirloom, huh? According to the engraving here the ring's only about two years old," said Eddie.

"Engraving?"

"Take a look," he said holding out his magnifying glass.

Lizzie took the glass and looked at the inside of the ring. It said, "For BW 1997."

"Whatta ya know," said Lizzie.

"I'll give you $500, which would bring your marker down to $34,500," said Eddie as he turned back to his eggs and hash and resumed eating.

"Five hundred! Those diamonds alone must be worth four thousand."

"So take it to a jeweler. I figure you come to me cause this baby might be a little warm."

"Forget it, Eddie. I made a mistake. You want some more coffee?"

"That would be lovely, doll."

"How about a thousand?"

"Seven hundred."

"You're still a scumbag, aren't ya Eddie?"

Lizzie was getting up from the booth when Eddie grabbed her by the wrist and squeezed.

"Let me tell you something, sweet pea. The people I have to deal with eat shitheads like you for breakfast. So let's get one thing straight. You came to me. The only reason I'm even wasting my time talking to you is because we got a history. So you think about it. You want me to take this hot potato off your hands and knock seven large off your note, I'll be in my office until six. Meanwhile, let me give you a little advice, Lizzie baby. We got some new players in town. Some boys from Bridgeport. They bought your debt, even though I still service it."

"What do you mean 'they bought my debt?' Who buys debt?"

"Hey, it's done all the time on Wall Street. Banks sell mortgages. It's the same with these guys. In case you ain't read the papers lately, there's been kind of a consolidation among certain East Coast family members. Anyway, what I'm saying, is that the sooner you clean up your note, the better. These boys have a rep. They play rough. They're gonna want their regular weekly payments, not blowjobs, know what I'm saying?"

"What if I pay off everything I owe? Can you give me a little more on the ring?"

"Tell ya what, sweetheart. You show up at six with the thirty-five grand, I'll give you eight for the ring. That's the best I can do. Now how about some more coffee?"

15

DETECTIVE ROY MCCARTHY sat in his Crown Victoria and stared at the yellow ranch house, with the attached two-car garage. Inside the house was a six-year-old girl. She was the last person in the world he wanted to see right now. What do you say to a kid whose mother was found dead in her kitchen and that the person responsible could be her father? Have you seen your daddy, by the way? We're sort of looking for him.

It took the Huntington Police nearly a day to track down the daughter, who apparently had been staying with the victim's sister when the death occurred. They couldn't even call it murder yet because the finding by the medical examiner was inconclusive. After all, Huntington, Long Island hadn't had a real official murder in 17 years, something the Chief of Police had impressed upon Roy when he took the job four months earlier. Before that, Roy had spent eight years in the high crime section of West Cranston, Long Island, on the southern shore where there was a homicide or two every month. Most of them were drug- or gang-related. There were no gangs in Huntington, and that was just fine with Roy. Roy hated gangs. Having grown up in Brooklyn, he'd been surrounded by one gang or another his entire childhood. They mostly left him alone, since he refused to join. Every now and then they'd bully him, or shake him down for protection money. What he hated most about them was what they did to his friends. As soon as a friend joined a gang, that was the end of their friendship. They could no longer associate with anyone who was not a gang member, so that left Roy out. He spent most of his high school years alone. After two years of college, he joined the biggest gang of all, the New York City Police Department. That was 32 years ago.

Now, one year away from retirement, he sat in his car looking at the yellow ranch house and felt alone again, even though he shared the car with Felicia Davenport. She was a 31-year-old detective junior grade who'd scored points with Roy when she refused two thousand dollars to pose nude for a men's magazine doing a spread on the female side of Long Island's finest. She was a lot prettier than the policewomen who did take the money and shed their blues. They were a disgrace to the force, as far as Roy was concerned.

"How about it Roy, are we going in, or what?" she asked when she realized her partner wasn't moving to get out of the car.

"I was just thinking," said Roy. "What kind of man kills his wife, calls 911, then runs away, leaving a six-year-old daughter behind?"

"A scared kind of man," said Felicia. "Let's get it over with."

"You read the initial M.E.'s report?"

"Twice," said Felicia. "Don't get it, though. How'd she die?"

"Berry aneurysm."

"Right. What's a Berry aneurysm?"

"A blood vessel in the brain ruptured."

"He must have hit her pretty hard to cause that."

"Yeah, well we're still waiting for the final report."

"What's that supposed to mean?"

"Means we want to make sure before we charge him that him striking her is what killed her."

"Couldn't the D.A. charge him with plain old assault and boot it up to homicide later?"

"He could, but this guy's running for office this year and wants everything to be nice and tidy. We should get a final report in a couple days. But first I just want to find this guy."

"You think his daughter knows where he is?"

"You got any better ideas?"

"What are you going to tell her about her father?"

"Nothing. I figure I'll let you do that."

"Oh, no."

"Come on, Felicia. What do you think I asked you to come along for?"

"Because you like looking at my legs."

"That too."

"You owe me, Roy. Big time."

June Cutter was standing at her sink looking out the window at the big blue car sitting at the end of her driveway. It had to be them, she figured. June's eyes filled with tears as she turned away from the window just as her six-year-old niece entered the kitchen.

"When can I go home, Auntie June?"

June kneeled down so she could be eye level with her niece. "Lisa, honey. Oh baby."

"Are you crying?"

"Yes, I am."

"Why?"

"Lisa. Some policemen are going to come by and ask you some questions."

"Policemen? I didn't do anything wrong."

"No darling, you didn't do anything wrong. It's about your mother."

"Do they know when Mommy's coming back?"

"Lisa. I'm afraid your mommy isn't coming back," June sniffed back some more tears.

"Why not, Auntie June?"

"Something's happened to your mother, honey. She had an accident."

"What kind of accident?"

"A real bad one."

"Is my Mommy dead?"

"Yes, honey. I'm so very, very sorry."

The little girl's eyes filled with tears and she began to sob. June felt her own eyes well up as she pulled her niece to her. "Go on and cry, honey. Your mother was someone to cry over. She was the best."

After a moment, Lisa pulled away and wiped her eyes.

"Does Daddy know?"

Oh God, thought June as she felt her knees weaken. Give me the strength to get through this. She stood up and held on to the kitchen counter. "Honey, we don't know where your daddy is. That's why the police are coming by."

June looked out the window again and saw two people get out of the police car and start walking toward the house. One looked like he was in his 50s, slightly overweight, soft in the middle but with a kind-looking face. He looked like he'd make a better Santa Claus than a police detective. All he needed was the white beard, thought June. Trade in his tweed jacket, tan pants and maroon tie for a red suit and he'd be perfect.

He was followed by an attractive woman with a no-nonsense expression on her face, wearing a blue business suit.

June started toward the front door before she heard the chime.

"Good morning," she said opening the front door. "I'm June Cutter. Sally Wilson's sister."

"Detective McCarthy and this is Detective Davenport."

"Please, come on in."

They entered a spacious living room recently decorated in a Southwestern motif with dark red, black, and brown sofas and overstuffed arm chairs with brown leather accessories.

"Please. Have a seat. May I offer you some coffee or something?

"None for me, thanks," said Roy.

"Same here," said Felicia. "We don't want to take up any more of your time than necessary."

"We're sorry for your loss," said Roy.

"Thank you."

"Is the daughter here?" asked Felicia.

"I'll go get her."

June left the living room and returned to the kitchen.

"You really think she's gonna know anything?" asked Felicia.

"It never hurts to ask."

"You sure about that?" said Felicia as Lisa entered the living room with her aunt. The little girl looked scared.

"Does she know what happened?" asked Felicia.

"She knows her mother is dead and that's all."

"We're sorry about what happened to your mommy, Lisa," said Roy.

"What happened?" asked Lisa. "Was she in a car accident?"

Roy and Felicia exchanged a look. Felicia knelt down so she could look Lisa in the face. "No, your mother wasn't in a car accident. We're still trying to find out how she died."

"Is that why you want to find my daddy?" asked Lisa. "Do you think he knows?"

"Ah. Actually, that's exactly right. We think he could probably help in that regard."

"I don't know where he is," said Lisa.

"Well, where did he like to go? Was there a special place that you can remember?

"He liked to go to the movies."

"He did? That's great," said Felicia. "I like the movies, too. Anyplace else?"

"Hmmm," said Lisa, thinking.

"Did your daddy have any friends?" asked Roy.

"Just me and Mommy. We were his friends."

"How about trips. Did your father ever take you on any trips?" said Felicia.

"You mean like Disneyland?"

"Did your father ever talk about any place special that he might have gone to when he was your age?"

Lisa made a face, trying to remember. Then her eyes widened. "When Daddy was little, he said his parents couldn't afford to take him to places like Disney World, so his mommy and daddy went to this lake. They made him wear an orange life preserver before he could go in the water "

"Did he say where this lake was?"

"Somewhere in Connecticut."

"Did he say what part of Connecticut?"

"I don't remember."

"Wait," said June. "I think I know what she's talking about. Sally mentioned it once. Lakeside? It was supposed to be real nice. They used to rent cottages on a lake there, but I don't think you can anymore. Do you think he might have gone there?"

"It's a long shot, but right now it's all we've got. Thank you, Mrs. Cutter. And thank you, Lisa."

"Are you gonna find my Daddy?" asked Lisa.

"We're sure gonna try," said Roy, writing something in his notebook.

"If you see him, tell him I miss him."

"I bet he misses you, too," said Roy, looking down at the little girl with sadness in his eyes.

When they got back in their car, Roy let out a deep sigh. He put his notebook on the seat between them.

"I'll have his photo faxed to the police in Lakeside," said Felicia.

"I'm going up there," said Roy.

"Why?" asked Felicia. "He might not even be there. I'll fax them his photo. They can contact us when they pick him up and we can go up together."

"What else am I gonna do? Sit around here and wait? You got my beeper. Anything comes in, beep me."

"I take it that means you don't want me along."

"I don't think the Chief would be too happy if we both went."

Roy looked back at the ranch house and started the car.

"Why are you doing this?" asked Felicia.

"Doing what?"

"Goin' after him if we can't even arrest the guy, yet."

"I guess I want to find him before anything else happens."

"Like what?"

"I don't know. The guy's on the run. He may have killed his wife. Who knows what he'll do? All I know is that for some people once they kill, it's never hard for them to do it again. He may feel like he's got nothing left to lose. Besides, you saw that little girl. I'm gonna try to get her daddy back alive. Losing one parent is hard enough on a kid. But two? Even if he goes to jail, she'll still be able to visit him. But if he's on the run, and feeling guilty, he might try to take his own life."

"When did you become such a softie?"

"I'll let you know where I am. If that coroner's final report comes in while I'm up there, beep me."

"Be careful."

"You can count on that."

"If he's gonna off himself, McCarthy, don't let him use you to do it, okay?"

"You got no worries there, babe. In my old precinct, we had a suicide-by-cop at least once a week. It ain't gonna happen to me."

16

HE AWOKE with a start. There was a flutter in his heart as he shivered awake. Where was he now? He had been dreaming. Or at least he thought he'd been dreaming. He looked down at the surgical gown. In his dream, he'd been wearing a suit. A pinstriped suit. He closed his eyes and tried to recall the images. There he was, getting dressed for work. Which means he has a job. What does he do? He opened his eyes, then closed them again. Another image floated by. A paisley tie. Then a memory. The tie had been a gift, but from whom? Who gave him the tie? "Who am I?" he shouted, then opened his eyes again and sat up. He was on an overstuffed chair in somebody's living room.

He was still above the restaurant. How long had he been asleep? He got up and looked around. There must be a clock around somewhere. He found the bedroom and saw an alarm clock next to the bed. It was nearly eleven. It's still light outside so that means it's eleven in the morning.

He couldn't stay there. The owner could return at any time. He needed something to wear. Quickly, he opened a closet and began trying on clothes. Nothing fit right. The pants were too wide and too short. The shirtsleeves barely covered his long arms. The shoes were three sizes too small. Thongs. They were better than trying to squeeze into shoes that were too small. At least he'd be able to walk. If he wore the pants low on his hips with a belt he could almost pass. But the shirts. He then went to the dresser and opened a drawer. T-shirts. That might work. He looked until he found one that didn't have a hole in it and some kind of awful stain that refused to come out in the wash. He checked himself in the mirror. Okay, he wouldn't win any fashion prizes but he would blend in, at least among the grunge crowd, if there was such a thing.

He still needed money. I've become a thief now. Whoever you are, I promise I'll pay you back for the clothes and any money I find. Maybe I should leave a note. Forget the note. Just find some money and get out of there. Where would he keep his money? How about in a bank, stupid. Who leaves money lying around? I do. Or I did, didn't I? I don't know. It sounds familiar. A stash of cash for emergencies. Money. Where would I hide money? The sock drawer. Nope, just socks. In a box somewhere. There's a box on the dresser. Would anyone be stupid enough to leave money there? He opened the box and there was a loose pile of bills and change, fives ones and quarters. He quickly counted it and it came to $23.75. I will pay back every cent. I promise you. With interest, as soon as I find out who I am and where I bank.

107

He stuffed the money in a pants pocket and then went into the bathroom to check his head wound. Looking in the mirror, he gently removed the green surgical cap that covered the blood-soaked bandages wrapped around his partially shaved head. Closing his eyes, he lifted the bandage and then looked. But what he saw was an explosion of blinding, bright light. Then, as if he was watching a movie playing backwards in slow motion, the light disappeared, and he saw the muzzle of a gun pointed right at him. That's it. He'd been shot. But why?

He squeezed his eyes shut. "Come on," he said. "Show me. Show me who shot me." But the blinding light exploded in his mind along with an excruciating pain that made him dizzy. He gripped the sink and opened his eyes. The room had turned blurry and he thought he was going to pass out again from the pain. He quickly pushed two more painkillers into his mouth, turned on the cold tap and cupped his hands under the faucet. He shoved handfuls of water into his mouth and swallowed the pills. He immediately took two more, then opened the medicine cabinet and took all the bottles of painkillers he could find and stuffed them in his baggy pants. He looked back at the mirror and studied the face that stared back at him. "Who are you? Who shot you?" A notion rumbled through his empty mind. He reached into a pocket, felt a crumpled piece of paper. He covered the paper in his fist and pulled it from the pocket. Looking down, he opened his hand and saw the crumpled paper was a five-dollar bill. Thoughts surged through his aching head. "Money?" he asked himself aloud. It had something to do with money. Is that why they shot me? To take my money?

A creaking sound caught his attention. The stairs. Someone was coming up the back stairs. He turned off the bathroom light and quietly slid down the hall. The sound of footsteps was on the back porch, then, "That sonofabitch," yelled the familiar voice of the restaurant owner. He then heard the sound of broken pieces of glass being shoved aside. He slid along the wall until he came to another door. He could hear the back door creak as he opened the door next to him and stepped through. He was now outside, on a balcony overlooking the front of the restaurant. Directly in front of him stood the hospital and in front of the hospital were two police cars. But as he looked from side to side, he realized there was no way off the balcony except the door he just stepped through. He could hear the owner thrashing around inside his apartment, muttering. "Stupid cop. The prick *was* up here." He heard the back door slam and then it was quiet. He was about to go back inside when he looked down and saw the police officer who had missed him on the back porch talking to another officer next to a patrol car. He had to get out of there. As he ran to the back door, he saw one more piece of clothing he needed. It was a baseball cap with a UConn Huskies logo over the brim. At least it would cover the large scab and the shaved strip around his head.

He went down the stairs and peeked around the corner of the building. The restaurant owner was walking across the street toward the two patrolmen. The owner was shaking his fist and screaming something at the officer who came into the restaurant. The officer looked up to the apartment over the restaurant and then reached into the patrol car and pulled out a handheld mike.

The Stranger ducked back around and started to walk away from the building. He had to make it across the empty lot before they returned. As he walked, he looked down and realized the thongs were making distinct tracks in the dirt. They would be on his tail in no time. He bent down and removed the thongs, then leaped from the trail onto a patch of tall grass. Walking barefoot, he scampered sideways across the lot but in another direction. He came to a street and put the thongs back on. As he was standing up, he looked over a bush at the back lot and there were the two police officers following the tracks across the lot but away from where he was standing. He couldn't stay on the street for long. A few yards away, a bus was pulling into a bus stop. He walked over to the bus stop and got in line to board. He stepped aboard and the door closed behind him. He took out a dollar and the driver shook his head and nodded at the sign over the windshield. "Exact change or token."

"How much?"

"Seventy-five cents."

He took the only change he had and put it in the box next to the driver. The bus pulled away just as the police officers stepped through bushes, splitting up, each walking in a different direction down the street.

He had to get out of this place, but how far would $23 take him? And where would he go? He took a seat by the window and stared out at the world moving by. What was this place called? The truck driver told him. Lake something. A picture of a boy at the edge of the water, in red trunks, with a pail and plastic shovel. The smell of old cabin wood. Lakeside. That's where I am. And I've been here before. Do I live here? How come nothing looks familiar? All these questions and no answers. You've been shot in the head, for God's sake. Maybe you're dead. No. People see you. In fact, the police are after you. So you're alive. But shot in the head. That explains why you can't remember anything. The bullet must have wiped out your memory. Still, there are traces of something. That boy by the lake. Was that me?

Suddenly the bus came to a halt. "Last stop. Lakeside train station."

Stepping out of the bus, he shielded his eyes from the bright noon sunlight. The train station was a two-story wooden structure with a narrow walkway on the second floor stretching above the tracks to the other side. There was a small white sign over the door that said "New York Side," which meant the trains on the near tracks went toward New York City. This being a Saturday, there were only a few people waiting for a train. A couple of mothers with their children, and some teenagers. He started to walk toward the ticket counter when he stopped. Standing off to the side and watching anyone who bought a ticket, was a policeman. He inconspicuously turned to study the front page of the local newspaper in one of the honor boxes. No headlines about someone being robbed or shot in the head. The only picture was that of a lonely lifeguard on a beach with a sign that read "No Swimming." The picture was under a headline: "Pollution Keeps Area Beaches Closed."

When he looked up he saw a little girl staring at him. Actually, she was looking at the side of his head. He reached up and felt the wetness. A small trickle of blood had leaked out from under the bandage. Trying not to draw attention, he walked slowly away from the train station. As he walked, he wiped away the blood with the back of his hand and pressed the cap to his head to staunch the bleeding.

He needed something to clean away the blood. As he walked down the street he came to a convenience store. He bought a package of tissues and cleaned the remaining blood from his temple and cheek. A wave of hunger caused him to stop and lean against the outside of the store.

He was pressing a wad of tissues against the wound when the store owner stepped outside and looked at him.

"You can't stand there," said the owner.

"No problem. Is there a restaurant around here?"

"Lakeside Diner. Two blocks that way."

"Thanks," he said and pushed away from the wall.

Folding the remaining tissues into a pad, he wedged it under the cap and on top of the blood-soaked bandage. The pad quickly turned red but managed to stop the leakage.

As he walked along, he realized he not only needed food, but that he had to use the bathroom.

The Lakeside Diner was like something out of another time. It was the old railroad car design, long and narrow. It had metal siding, but instead of the usual silver, someone had painted it a dark green. There were about a half-dozen cars parked in front. Across the street was a Burger King and its lot was full. Not hard to guess who got the lunchtime crowd around here. Still, he didn't feel like fighting a crowd for a hamburger, so he entered the diner.

The first thing that hit him was the smoke. It seemed like half the people eating at the counter had a cigarette in their hands. This wasn't going to work. At the end of the diner, he saw a sign that said "Restrooms." He made his way to the restroom, holding his breath until he got there. Closing the door behind him, he took a deep breath and almost gagged. The pungent smell of urine almost brought tears to his eyes. He looked down at the toilet and saw that whoever had been there before him had managed to soak the seat and splatter the wall and floor on each side.

As soon as he emptied his bladder, he zipped up, washed his hands and left the room. Burger King it was. He started to head for the front door when he heard a female voice behind him shout out, "Hey. The toilets are supposed to be for the customers."

That voice. He'd heard that voice before. He started to turn around to see who it belonged to when a male voice shouted out from the kitchen. "Lizzie. You got a phone call."

Suddenly he froze. Lizzie? Did he know a Lizzie? He turned to see what she looked like but all he could see was her back as she walked around the counter. Just then, the front door opened and two men tried to enter, but he was blocking their way.

"You coming or going, pal?" asked the taller of the two.

"Sorry," he said as he stepped outside.

He looked back through one of the many windows along the side and saw the woman start to pick up a phone receiver. But she still had her back to him. He moved further along the outside of the diner until he came to a window that gave him a better view. But now the receiver covered the only part of her face he could see. He would just have to wait until she finished talking and turned around.

Lizzie held the receiver tight to her ear so she could hear over the noise of the diner. "Hello."

"I know what you did," said a muffled male voice.

A worried look washed over her face as she glanced around the diner to see if anyone was watching. She pulled the phone closer to her.

"Who is this?" she whispered.

"I want ten thousand dollars in cash. Twenties and fifties," said the muffled voice. "You've got 12 hours. Leave the money in the dumpster behind the Burger King. If it's not there by midnight tonight, the next call goes to the Lakeside Police."

Wait, thought Lizzie. I know that voice. "Paul? Is that you?"

The line went dead.

"That little bastard," she said to no one as she hung up the phone, turned around and headed back to her customers. She didn't see the face of the Stranger in the window on the outside of the diner.

17

HE FELT LIKE he'd been punched in the heart. It was her. He put a hand over his mouth to stop the raging roar that was rising out of the depths of his fury. Immediately, he felt dizzy and reached out to steady himself. Suddenly, it was all coming back to him in a roller coaster adrenaline rush of jumbled emotions and events whirling together. He closed his eyes and saw tiny dots of moving lights. He was on a dance floor and she was looking up at him. Those dark, violet-blue eyes. They seemed to suck him into her inner world. A world that she controlled. It was like he was in a trance. He could feel himself getting erect right there on the dance floor. Then they were outside and her tongue was in his mouth, while her hands massaged him through his pants. He had no will. She was in total control and he didn't care.

But why didn't he care? What had he done? The answer exploded in his mind, causing him to lose his balance and fall to the ground beneath the diner's window.

The Stranger trembled as scenes began to flash back, attacking all his senses. New scenes. From another time and another place. Before the night of dancing in that strange bar with that woman. There was that tie again. It must be earlier in the day. But what day? Yesterday? The day before. What day is it now?

He was standing before a mirror, tying a paisley tie. Behind him was a woman in a pink robe. He could hear himself say, "Now? Can't this wait until tonight?"

"It won't take long," said the woman in the robe. "I sent Lisa over to my sister's so we could have this time to talk."

In the reflection, he could see the sadness on her face, but he had more important things on his mind. He had to get somewhere. His office. Some important meeting.

"But I'm already running late," he said, kissing her on the forehead, then bending down to pick up his briefcase. He was walking toward the bedroom door when he heard the words.

"I want a divorce."

The words echoed off the canyons of his mind. He saw himself turning around and putting down his briefcase.

"At least I got your attention," said the woman, letting out a deep sigh.

"My attention? Is that what this is about? Look, I can't be late."

"Didn't you hear me? I want out."

"Out of what? Our marriage?"

"I didn't think it was going to be like this," she said, her eyes brimming with tears as a few rolled down her cheeks.

"Be like what?"

"I didn't think I was going to be alone so much."

"Alone? When are you alone? What about Lisa?"

Who was Lisa? The woman looked right into his eyes and said, "What about her? I feel like a single parent already. Might as well make it official."

She must be our daughter.

"I can't believe you're doing this," he heard himself say. "Especially now. Next year's bonuses are being determined at this meeting. Do you know what it means if I'm late?"

"You better get going then," replied the woman who must be his wife.

He picked up his briefcase and walked to the kitchen. He stopped and turned toward his wife who had followed him.

"That's not fair. I work for what we have. This house. Our cars."

"You said the salesman job was a rite of passage. That you'd be off the road and in an office with regular hours in no time. Remember saying that? That was ten years ago. Just this year you've been away more than you've been home. I thought we agreed we would both raise Lisa."

"I can't help it if my company's gone global. Don't I try to bring you and Lisa along on as many trips as possible? But how would it look if I'm the only salesman whose wife and kid came along to Hong Kong and London? Wait a second. Okay. I get it. Who is it?"

"Who's what?"

"Who are you having an affair with?"

"You think that's what this is about?"

"I just hope it isn't somebody we know, somebody I have to face."

"You are such an asshole. What makes you think I'm having an affair?"

"It's the only explanation that makes any sense."

For a moment they both stared at each other, like two different breeds of dogs, encountering each other without their leashes or their masters, deciding whether to attack or run off.

"I just want what I'm entitled to," she said, breaking the silence. "Half the value of the house, my car. We'll split the bank accounts."

"What if I say 'no?' What about Lisa? How could you do this?"

"It's suddenly all my fault."

"You're the one talking about destroying the family. What if I refuse?"

"I've already talked to a lawyer. You can't stop me. All you can do is make it more painful than it has to be."

"Painful for who? Goddamn you Sally!" he shouted, throwing his briefcase to the floor. Ahah. My wife's name is Sally, he thought. But what's my name?

The scene continued to unfold.

"If you think I'm just gonna sit back and let this happen, you're wrong," he heard himself say. "I've worked too hard for this. I suppose you expect me to just pack up and leave, too. Well, this is my home. I'm not going to be one of those guys who's broke and living in a furnished studio apartment in some pay-by-the-month hotel while his ex-wife and her lover live it up on his money. It's not gonna happen to me."

"Fine," said Sally. "I'll find a place."

"So you admit it."

"Admit what?"

"Just tell me who it is. Come on. Who's the lucky guy?"

"Fuck you."

He remembered feeling the rage rushing through his body, up his chest and shoulders and down his arm as he pulled back. Then he remembered slamming her with his open palm, striking her on the side of her face, a full hand

117

blow from her temple to her chin. The loud smack reverberated through the kitchen and his hand stung from the impact.

The blow hit Sally so fast and hard that it knocked her off her balance. She reached out to grab a counter to keep from falling, but her hand missed and she fell sideways, slamming her head onto the sharp corner of the counter as she collapsed onto the floor. Her feet slid out from under her and the back of her head came down hard on the tile floor. Then she blinked twice. Her left leg twitched and suddenly, she was still.

"Goddamn it. Now look what you made me do," he said kneeling down next to his wife. He took her left arm and shook it. "Sally. Wake up. Come on. I'm sorry. I shouldn't have slapped you. But damn. Can't we talk about this?"

She lay motionless. He leaned in close and listened for a breath, a heartbeat.

"Sally?"

He put a hand on her neck and felt for a pulse. He pushed down on her chest, then pulled her mouth open and put his mouth over hers and blew in. He pulled his mouth away and pushed on her chest again. Then went back to her mouth and blew more in. He did this ten more times until he was out of breath.

"Oh, God. No."

He stood up and let out a sigh. He saw the cordless phone lying on the counter next to the 13-inch television. He picked it up and punched in 911. When an operator picked up he said, "There's been an accident. My wife's been hurt. She isn't moving. Please come to 15 Maple Lane."

He hung up the phone and knelt back down to the floor. "Sally, please. Forgive me."

Then, as if he was in a trance, he stood up, and walked out of the kitchen. Quickly, he vaulted up the beige carpeted stairs of the eight-year-old colonial, taking two steps at a time, and into the master suite. He opened the top drawer of his custom-made walnut bedroom dresser and removed his passport. Then he opened the wall safe hidden behind a painting that hung over a king-size bed and took out an envelope. He checked the envelope, his emergency stash.

Should he pack a suitcase? No time. How long would it take for the police to arrive? He had to move quickly. Maybe he should just wait there. Face the music. He killed his wife. He should be punished. But what about Lisa? How could he ever face her?

He remembered getting into his car and driving away, hearing the siren of the emergency medical vehicle in the distance. He drove without direction. He drove until the road ended at the Montauk lighthouse, then turned around and drove back. But he couldn't go back. The life he had been living up until this morning had ended. He had killed his wife and he did not deserve to live. That, he now realized, was why he didn't care. He closed his eyes and the tears began to fall.

18

INSIDE THE DINER, Lizzie was trying to contain her anger over the phone call. The nerve of that little prick. She had already messed up two simple orders and knew that meant no tips from them. Goddamn Paul. What an asshole. She looked at the clock. It was 12:30. She had to call Julia and nip this little disaster in the bud. Who did that bastard think he was to threaten her like that? This had to be his pea-brain idea. Julia was too smart to pull anything like this. She felt in her pocket for a quarter and waited until Hector had his back to her. Then she walked over to the pay phone next to the restroom sign.

Julia was putting down a bag of groceries when the phone rang. She didn't feel like talking to anyone after the morning's unpleasantness. It had turned out the root canal had been a mistake, and that what Mrs. Pershing had actually required was oral surgery and periodontal work. Still, it might be Paul calling from the service station, so she left the groceries on the counter and picked up the phone on the third ring.

"Hello."

"It's me," said Lizzie.

"What's up? Why are you whispering?"

"I'm at the diner. I can't really talk now, but I get a break at two. Can you come here?"

"I thought we were going to stay clear of each other for a while," said Julia.

"Is Paul there?"

"No. Why?"

"Where is he?"

"At the station, I guess. What's this all about?"

"I'll tell you when I see you."

"Wait."

But Lizzie had already hung up.

Julia put the phone down and felt a chill. What had her husband done?

The Stranger was still lying face down on the ground next to the diner when he heard the front door open and close behind him. He looked over and saw the woman walking across the parking lot to a Jeep. He pulled his legs in and hid between a large thick bush and the wall of the diner. Tiny branches poked into his face, and scratched his cheeks. He watched as she opened a door on the passenger side of the jeep, reached in and pulled out a pack of cigarettes. The door opened again and a man in a white apron stepped out.

"Hey, Lizzie. I got four orders in here ready to go. You mind holding off that smoke until you serve our customers?"

Lizzie put her cigarette into the pack and walked back toward the diner. "You're just moving too fast for me, Hector."

After she went back inside, the Stranger let out a breath. She might know who he is. But she was the one who shot him. There was somebody with her. Her husband. That's right. She lured him out to his car, and then the husband showed up. They were trying to blackmail him. But why did she shoot him? He remembered deciding to give her the gun back, but then it went off. There was a blinding white explosion and then blackness until he felt the water in his nose. They drove his car into the lake with him in it. They thought he was dead and were trying to bury him. He had money in that car. Would they have taken the money? They would if they found it. He had to assume they did, which meant they might still have it. He needed that money to get away.

Her address would be on the registration in the Jeep. But what if she sees you? It's a chance you'll just have to take. He looked into the window and saw that she had her back to the front, and was talking to the cook.

It's now or never. He walked quickly to the Jeep, opened the passenger-side door and climbed inside. He opened the glove compartment and found an insurance card and registration. There it is: 67 Cherry Orchard Lane, Lakeside.

He put the card and registration back in the glove compartment and was about to get out of the Jeep when he saw an emergency can of gasoline behind the backseat. These people tried to kill him. He sat back down and for the first time in as long as he could remember, he felt a smile coming on.

Lizzie was dying for a cigarette. Was it her imagination, or was the second hand on the clock over the door moving slower? "How 'bout some more coffee over here?" Lizzie picked up the half-filled coffeepot and walked past the counter when a flash of bright orange light glared through the front windows, along with a loud whooshing sound. Lizzie looked up and dropped the coffeepot on the floor. Shattered glass and hot coffee flew in all directions.

"Jesus, Lizzie!" yelled Hector.

But Lizzie was already running to the front door.

"Where do you think you're going?"

But then Hector looked over her shoulder as she threw open the front door.

"Holy shit!" he yelled, and quickly followed her outside.

In the parking lot, Lizzie's Jeep was a ball of fire. Flames were shooting out all four open windows. Lizzie was walking toward it in a state of shock when Hector grabbed her from behind and pulled her away, just as the gas tank exploded. The blast lifted the Jeep off the ground, turning it into a twisted wreck of rubber and metal.

19

THE STRANGER was across the street eating in the Burger King when the police cars and fire trucks arrived. The Jeep had burned down to a skeletal frame by the time the firemen doused the blaze with thick white foam. He looked at the address he'd written down and then walked to a pay phone near the rear entrance. He called information and asked for a local cab company and then asked to be connected. The dispatcher told him a car would arrive in ten minutes, so he returned to his table and watched the excitement across the street.

As he sat back down, he saw a pickup truck pull into the diner's parking lot. Then another familiar figure got out of the passenger side and the truck pulled away. It was her husband. The man with the video camera. He looked down at the address. At least he was sure the house would be empty.

John started across the parking lot when he nearly slipped on the foam the firemen had used to douse the flames. Walking around a wide puddle of foam, he continued on to Lizzie who was leaning against the hood of another car, smoking a cigarette.

"Jesus, Lizzie. What happened?

Lizzie turned toward John and gave him a deadpan look. She took a deep drag. "What's it look like, Einstein? Somebody torched our fucking Jeep."

"Who'd do a thing like that?"

She ground out the remainder of her cigarette and walked over to the smoking wreckage. "Somebody with access to gasoline."

"What's that supposed to mean?"

"I got a call."

"What kind of call?"

"Blackmail."

"Shit. Somebody knows?"

"Come over here. I don't want to have to shout."

Lizzie walked John out of earshot of the crowd gathered around the smoldering Jeep.

"Paul called me."

"Paul? Our Paul?"

"He tried to disguise his voice, but I'm sure it was him."

"You think he did this?" he asked, nodding toward the Jeep.

"I don't know."

"What did he say?"

"He wanted ten thousand dollars by midnight. In small bills."

"How'd he find out about the money?"

"I don't know. I didn't say anything. Did you?"

"Fuck no."

"Then maybe he was just guessing."

"I don't get it. Why would he torch your Jeep after just blackmailing you? That doesn't make any sense."

"I let him know that I knew who it was. Maybe he did this to throw us off."

"It's all too weird. What about Julia? Does she know about this?"

"I don't think so. But she's on her way over here for a chat."

"If Paul did this I'll kill the sonofabitch."

"Just take it easy. We need more information. Let me talk to Julia, see if she knows anything. We don't want to let things get out of control here."

"I'd say things have already gotten out of control, Lizzie. That Jeep wasn't insured."

"Well, whose fault was that, asshole? Where's Brian? You were supposed to be watching him."

"I dropped him off with your grandmother."

"She let you?"

"I told her I had a job interview. What are we gonna do about this blackmail stuff?"

"We're not gonna do anything. Paul's not gonna call the police. Even he's not that stupid."

"I wouldn't be too sure," said John. "The police talk to you yet about the Jeep?"

"Told them I have no idea who might have done it. I was in the diner working when it happened. They think it's one of the loan sharks we owe money to just making a statement."

"You told the police we owed money to loan sharks?"

"Didn't have to. That bright young police officer over there taking eye witness statements figured it out all by himself."

"Well, I hope you told him he was wrong?"

"Don't worry. I didn't give him any names."

"Lizzie. You don't want the police pissing off those guys, or they'll do worse than trash our Jeep."

"Well, I figure we will have paid them off before that happens."

"Where is that money, anyway?" asked John.

"It's in a safe place."

"Not the Jeep, I hope."

"Don't try to figure it out, John. It's just gonna give you a headache. By the way. The most we can get from Eddie for the ring is $700."

"That's robbery," said John.

"I can always tell him no."

"We'll take it. Most of the money's going to the loan sharks anyway. We'll need whatever we can get. Here comes our babe in her Buick."

Lizzie turned around and watched Julia pull into the parking lot and stop as far away from the fire truck and burned wreckage as she could get.

"What happened?" asked Julia, walking toward Lizzie and John. "Oh, my God. That's your Jeep!"

"Was our Jeep. Got any ideas?" asked Lizzie.

Julia looked at Lizzie with a mixture of anger and confusion.

"Why would I have any ideas?"

"You seen your husband lately?"

Julia glared at Lizzie but bit her lower lip at the same time.

"You know something," said Lizzie, walking closer to Julia. "She knows something, John."

"What? I don't know anything. Honest."

"Then how come when I asked you about Paul you did that thing with your lip there?" asked Lizzie. "Honey, we've been friends since ninth grade. I know every twitch, every smirk, every reaction you got, baby, and they all

127

mean something. Now what has that scumbag husband of yours been up to?"

"Paul's at work. Wait. You don't think *he* did this!"

"What do you think?"

"This is crazy."

"Yeah? So's setting fire to our Jeep."

"What makes you think Paul would ...."

"He called me, okay?" said Lizzie. "He threatened us, that if we didn't give him ten thousand dollars, he'd call the police. Do me a favor. Tell him it didn't work, and if he pulls another stunt like that I'll nail his balls to his asshole. All I want to know, is, did you know he was gonna do this?"

"I don't believe it."

"Believe it. He called me. Think about it. Who else could it be? Nobody else knows. Just us four. I know Paul's voice, Julia. He tried to disguise it, but he didn't do a very good job."

"There's one other person," said John.

"Who?" said Lizzie.

"The poor guy at the bottom of the reservoir," smiled John. "But then I don't think he'll be telling anyone."

Lizzie was looking at Julia as John spoke and saw something shift in her expression. Julia tried to cover it with an awkward smile.

"Julia," said Lizzie. "We need to know where you are on this."

"On what?"

"On what your husband's trying to do. The blackmail."

"I don't know anything about any blackmail," said Julia. "And I still don't believe Paul would do something like that."

"Well, he did," said Lizzie.

"What about our Jeep?" asked John. "Somebody's fuckin with us Julia. And right now all signs point to your dink-head husband."

128

"I can't believe this," said Julia.

"Let's put it this way, Julia," said Lizzie. "If it wasn't Paul, then we're all in a shitload of trouble."

"What do you mean?"

"It means somebody else knows."

"Who?"

"You tell us," said John.

"Okay," said Julia. "Let's say it was Paul. Maybe he was playing a joke."

"This ain't very fuckin funny," snapped John.

"I know," said Julia. "Let me talk to him. I'm going over to the gas station now. If he did what you say he did then he owes you both a big apology."

"Maybe we should all go talk to him."

"No. Let Julia go alone."

"I'd rather look him in the eye myself," said John.

"They'll be plenty of time for that," said Lizzie. "Besides, we're all still friends, aren't we Julia?"

"Sure," said Julia.

"You really trust her that much?" asked John.

"Julia and I trust each other, don't we baby?"

Julia nodded. "I'll call you," she said and walked to her Buick.

After Julia left, Lizzie turned to John. "She knows something. But I don't think she had anything to do with the Jeep or her husband's stupid blackmail call."

"What is it then?"

"I don't know. All I know is that it worries me."

"I thought you said you trusted her."

"Oh, I do. In fact, she's probably the only person I do trust."

"Other than me, you mean."

"Of course, darling. You know, if Paul is at the service station, then he couldn't have burned the Jeep."

"Jesus, Lizzie. Who then?"

"Eddie said something that I didn't really pay much attention to."

"What?"

"He sold our loan to some guys in Bridgeport."

"You think it was them?"

"I don't know. I don't know what to think."

"What are we gonna do?"

"Right now, we're gonna see if one of these fine young police officers can give us a lift home."

20

DETECTIVE ROY MCCARTHY drove past the "Welcome to Connecticut" sign on the New England Thruway, also known as I-95. The first exit was for a town called Byram. As he drove by, it occurred to him that while he had worked in the New York area for more than twenty years he had never heard of Byram. He knew about Greenwich, and Stamford and Westport and even Lakeside. But he didn't know anyone who lived in Byram. It was then that he realized this was the first time he'd ever had reason to travel into Connecticut.

He checked a notepad suction-cupped to the dash and saw that Lakeside was Exit Nine. The following three exits went to different sections of Greenwich, followed by another three exits to Stamford. Exit Nine was actually the eastern border of Stamford, but the sign said it was also the exit for Lakeside. McCarthy put on his directional and began to ease his Crown Victoria into the right lane. A huge tractor-trailer wasn't making it easy for him. He let up on the accelerator and let the sixteen-wheeler pass by before edging over. He was thankful that he didn't have to battle these whales on wheels every morning just to get to work.

He came to the end of the exit ramp and checked his notepad again. Turn left at stoplight. As he followed his instructions, he realized that I-95 ran right through the middle of Lakeside, along with the Metro North Railroad tracks. He passed over the six-lane highway and came to a wide intersection, designated Route 1, where he turned right and drove six blocks to the Lakeside Police Station.

Lakeside reminded him of Huntington. Both had a small downtown area, branching out from a main street surrounded by a variety of residential areas. Each had houses of different price levels and prestige along with the promise that life here was going to be safer, healthier and of an all-around higher quality than in a scrunched up and dirty, big bad city. The price for all that higher quality of life? A mortgage and a mind-altering commute that sucked four hours a day out of your life.

Roy turned into the entrance of the parking area in front of the Lakeside Police Station and parked in a visitor's spot. Turning off the car, he realized it had only taken him an hour and twenty minutes to drive from Huntington, Long Island to Lakeside, Connecticut. Yet, as he stepped out of the car to stretch, he felt as if he'd been driving for several hours. His back and joints ached from the tension of driving on the over-crowded highways and turnpikes that linked these two towns. There was also the added stress related to why he had even made the journey. What was he really doing here? How would he explain this to the Lakeside police chief who took his call but had questioned his motives? He'd read articles about the bond that often formed between the police and the criminal and how this symbiotic relationship sometimes affected the outcome of proper police procedure. It was the same kind of bond that formed between sports competitors. They shared a unique experience that no one else had shared and it was this sharing, the psychologists believed, that caused the bond to form. There was also a more basic connection in the fact that without the criminal there would be no need for the policeman, which meant each law enforcement officer owed his existence to the criminal he was pursuing.

Roy took in a deep breath and entered the public entrance to the Lakeside Police Station. There was a narrow lobby area with seats to the right and left and a reception counter directly in front. On a wall to the left was a glass cabinet with various awards and certificates. The wall to the right held a large wooden plaque with brass nameplates, each bearing the name of an officer killed in the line of duty. The detective's eyes were immediately drawn to the plaque. He counted four names of men who had died over the past 50-plus years of fighting crime in Lakeside. It held two more names than the one in the Huntington Police Department.

Eventually, he made his way to the reception counter and told the duty officer he was there to see Chief Manzini. He still didn't know what he was going to say to explain his visit.

Five minutes later a door to the right and next to the reception counter opened and an oval-shaped man in shirtsleeves stuck his head out. "Detective McCarthy?"

Roy stood up and followed the man through the door into an open office setting of numerous cubicles in the center and larger offices around side. Across the room against the back wall was the communications center, which housed the emergency 911 service as well as the dispatcher and other computer, facsimile and communications equipment. This layout was the exact opposite of McCarthy's station house, which had the communications center in front. Other than that, it could have been designed by the same architect.

Chief Manzini was sitting behind his desk in a large corner office. He was nearly bald, and wore rimless glasses that seamed to have a rose colored tinge to the lens. If McCarthy had to guess, he'd say the chief was in his 50s, in pretty good shape and probably didn't know a lot of jokes. McCarthy stood in front of the desk until Manzini looked up from whatever he was reading and nodded to one of the two chairs in front of his desk. He sat down and waited as Chief Manzini continued reading, then closed a folder, and removed his glasses.

"So, Detective McCarthy. Tell me again what brings you to our little town."

Roy cleared his throat and took out a folder with several eight-by-ten photographs. "This fella, here." He slid the pictures across the desk to Manzini who snatched them up, studied them for all of nine seconds and slid them back.

"His name is Bruce Wilson. We think he may be here in Lakeside," said McCarthy.

"What was it he did?"

"We think he may have killed his wife."

"May. That means you don't have enough to arrest him with."

"We're working on it. Right now, I just want to bring him in for questioning. He apparently made a 911 call and then fled the scene."

"Where his wife was killed."

"Right. There's evidence of a struggle. It appears someone struck her and that she hit her head on the kitchen counter. We're still waiting for the final autopsy report."

"But you think he did it."

"I do. There's no evidence yet of a third party. We have his voice on the 911 tape. If he didn't kill her, why did he run?"

"Good point. You could at least charge him with assault to hold him."

"That's up to the DA."

"So let me see if I understand this correctly. You drove all the way up here from Huntington, Long Island, to find somebody who may or may not even be here."

"I had nothing better to do."

"Why didn't ya just pick up the phone and tell us to pick him up? You could have faxed us his photo and we could have saved you a trip."

"He's got a little girl. I thought maybe I could expedite things a little if I came in person."

"He a friend of yours?"

"Never met the man."

Manzini gave McCarthy a suspicious look, drummed his fingers on his desk and then slid the envelope with the photos back across his desk so he could take one out. "Tell you what I can do, Detective McCarthy. In the interest of interdepartmental cooperation, I'll have some copies of his picture made and circulated. If he's in Lakeside, we'll find him."

"Thanks, Chief.

"There anything else I should know about this man? He got a record or anything?"

"Nothing."

"Give me your card and I'll call when we locate him."

"Actually, I thought I'd stay in town for the weekend, at least. Any modestly priced hotels you could recommend?"

"You don't think we can find him?"

"No. I'd just like to be here when you do."

"The Radisson down the street. Show them your shield and you'll get a 50% discount."

135

21

ORCHARD STREET was in one of Lakeside's lower-scale residential sections with tiny one-third acre lots and small three-bedroom houses. The street itself was lined with apple trees. The Stranger, Bruce Wilson, had picked and eaten about a half dozen small green apples by the time he reached a mailbox with the number 167 painted on it and his stomach had the cramps to prove it. He looked across a lawn and saw a rundown split level house with toys scattered across a lawn that was crying out to be mowed. He looked around to see if anyone was watching, then opened the mailbox. Reaching inside, he found a stack of letters and flyers. He pulled them out and looked at the names on the addresses. Bills were addressed to a John Daly. Some junk mail was addressed to an Elizabeth Daly.

Bruce put the letters back and closed the mailbox. Glancing around again, he slowly made his way to the front of the house and looked in through a dirty window. He pushed the doorbell and waited. No answer. He tried the door. It was locked. He then walked around the side of the house and found another door, also locked. In back of the house, he found a third entrance blocked by a stack of crushed cardboard boxes and pieces of lumber. He pushed the lumber and cardboard aside and tried the door. To his amazement, it opened and he slipped inside.

Who were these people, he wondered as he looked around the small kitchen and sink filled with unwashed dishes. Now that he was inside, he felt a wave of guilt. What was he doing here? He saw a stuffed figure on the floor of the kitchen. It was one of those wrestling buddy dolls. He then saw several small rubber wrestling figures. They must have a boy. He remembered the fad, but was thankful his daughter never felt compelled to stay up with all the other children who cajoled their parents into buying every pro-wrestling figure available. He found the refrigerator and instantly felt a pang of hunger.

Paul was cleaning the windshield on a silver Mercedes 500 when Julia pulled into the station going faster than she should. The car kicked up dust as she hit the brakes. He finished wiping the windshield as Julia bolted out of the car, slamming the door behind her. Paul gave the woman in the Mercedes her credit card and receipt and stole one last glance at the short skirt that had ridden half-way up the woman's thighs. He looked away just as Julia walked up behind him.

"Hey babe. What's up?"

"We have to talk," snapped Julia, waiting for the woman in her Mercedes to drive away.

"Wanta get some lunch?" asked Paul.

"What the hell has gotten into you?"

Paul started to back away as Julia got closer.

"Now just hold on a second."

"Hold on? Have you gone nuts?"

"I just wanted to shake her up a little."

"Shake her up? Oh, you shook her up all right. Paul, somebody could have gotten hurt."

"Hurt? Whatta ya talkin about?"

"Setting her Jeep on fire."

"Hey. I never set no Jeep on fire."

"Well, she thinks you did. She says you called her."

"But that's all, honest."

Julia looked deep in her husband's eyes, and then realized the truth with a jolt. "Oh God!" she blurted. "It must have been him."

"Who?"

"The man in the car. He's alive."

"It's gotta be somebody else."

"The only other possibility," said Julia, "is Eddie the Hand. Lizzie said they owed him some money."

"Now that makes sense."

"But your calling her doesn't make sense, Paul. How could you do something so stupid?

"I fucked up. I'm sorry."

"John's ready to rip you a new asshole. But Lizzie's the one you should be worried about."

"I'm not afraid of her."

"Well, you should be. As far as I know, John hasn't killed anybody yet. We have to tell her about the missing body."

"Why?"

"Because I don't think Eddie the Hand set their Jeep on fire."

"But you're the one who thought of him."

"Think about it. If they owe him money, wouldn't he just take the Jeep as partial payment? I think it's him."

"If it was, then that means he knows who she is."

"Maybe he knows about us, too," said Julia.

"Nah. How could he? It's her he's after. She's the one who shot him."

"We have to tell her," said Julia, heading for the pay phone in the station office.

"Wait a second," said Paul, reaching out and grabbing her by the arm. "Let's say he's really out there, stalking them. Why not just let it happen?"

"Let what happen?"

"Whatever. Just play it out."

"I can't do that."

"Why, because she's still your friend? She killed somebody and then forced us into helping her cover it up. She violated your friendship, Julia. Real friends don't do shit like that. She's dangerous."

"Which is another reason we should tell her the man she thought she killed might be alive. You don't know Lizzie like I do. If she finds out we knew he was alive and that we didn't tell her, I'd hate to think what she'd do."

"Like I said, she doesn't scare me," said Paul.

"Yeah? Then you're a bigger fool than I thought. Back in high school, Lizzie thought this other girl was making moves on this guy she was dating," said Julia. "So Lizzie broke into the girl's locker and soaked her tampons with spot remover. She had to be hospitalized for treatment of vaginal burns. Be scared, Paul."

Lizzie and John stood in the front door of their house staring at the mess someone had made of their living room. Chairs and sofas had been upturned, fabric ripped open. A bookshelf was lying on the floor with books sprayed out across the floor.

"Son of a bitch," said John.

Lizzie moved slowly through the wreckage and into the kitchen. She sniffed the air.

"Somebody's been cooking."

She found a soiled plate on the kitchen table next to an empty glass of milk. She felt the stove. "It's still warm."

She then opened the refrigerator and glared at what she saw.

"The fuckers ate our steaks."

John entered the kitchen with a white sock in his hand. "They also took about six hundred dollars out of my sock drawer."

"The money!" screamed Lizzie. She ran from the kitchen, down the hall and into the bathroom. Reaching behind the toilet, and under a loose tile, Lizzie lifted out the envelope she'd taken from the Lexus. She opened the envelope and quickly counted the money.

"You didn't get this, you bastards."

"I think it's time you gave your friend Eddie the Hand a call and tell him to pull off the goon squad or he won't get his money."

"It just doesn't make any sense," said Lizzie. "I told him we had the money. Why would they pull this shit now? There's something going on here, John. I don't think this is Eddie, or any mobsters from Bridgeport."

"What? You think Paul did this, too?"

"It's gotta be him. I told Julia the guy was a loser. She should never have married him. He's not getting away with it."

Since Bruce didn't have a credit card, the woman behind the desk said, the motel policy was to secure a $100 deposit with the balance returnable on check-out. That covered any additional expenses like long-distance calls, pay per view movies or whatever, she said with a crooked smile. Bruce handed her five 20s and she gave him a key chained to a green piece of plastic shaped like a tree with the words, Please return to Evergreen Motel, 299 East Main Street, Lakeside, CT, 06709.

The small, stifling room held the faint smell of stale cigarette smoke and Lysol disinfectant. There was barely enough room to maneuver since the bed nearly filled the entire space. Bruce tried to open a window, but it had been painted shut. A wave of depression mixed with anxiety pushed him down onto a worn mattress. Slowly, memories began to return, each one more painful than the next. He longed for the amnesia to return. He felt like he was in someone else's nightmare. Was this what life was going to be like from now on, this life on the run? Maybe he should just turn himself in. He didn't mean to kill his wife. It was an accident. He shifted his body off a broken spring that threatened to cut through the mattress cover. Maybe he could just impale himself on the curved jagged point of the bedspring. The guilt that was tearing him apart was overwhelming. He deserved to die. Why didn't he just let the black water take him? It would have been so easy. He had never been a religious man, yet he had the feeling something kept pulling him toward a greater purpose. It just wasn't his time and there was nothing he could do about it. He didn't ask to be born and therefore had no right to control his death. God must have a plan for him.

He rolled over and felt something crumble in his pocket. He turned on the lamp next to the bed and reached into his pocket. There was a stiff piece of paper or something with a sharp corner. Pinching it between two fingers, he pulled out the photo he took from the living room of the house that belonged to the couple who tried to blackmail him. He studied the picture under the light. Lizzie had her head leaning back against John's chest, and Julia was holding Paul's hand, a sad smile on her face. Bruce sat up and focused his attention on Julia. She was the one who refused to go along with the others. She had the face of an angel.

Lizzie was bent over the sofa, straightening the cushions when John came into the living room holding his pistol, checking the clip to make sure it was loaded. Lizzie stopped cleaning and stood up. "What are you doing?" she asked.

"I'm gonna pay your so-called best friend Julia and her rat hole husband a little visit."

"Put the gun away."

"Goddamnit, Lizzie. Look what he did. I'm gonna shoot his nuts off."

"The gun. Hand it over," she said, holding out her hand. John felt his manhood slip away as he reluctantly handed the weapon to his wife.

"You just let me take care of it, okay?" she said, slipping the pistol into her purse. "We have to be careful. It could be a trap to get us mad. Get us to go over there waving a gun around, and the police pop out."

"Those bastards!"

"Don't worry about Paul and Julia. I know how to handle them. It's you I'm worried about."

"Me?"

"You all right with all this?"

"How could you even ask such a question?"

"Cause you never talk about it."

"What's to talk about?"

"We gotta stay cool, John."

"I'm cool."

"Come here."

Lizzie took John by the hand and led him to the bedroom.

"What are you doing?" he asked.

"Just relax," she said. "We have a little time before Grandma drops off Brian."

"I don't think I could ...."

"Don't worry. You won't have to do anything," said Lizzie, unbuckling his jeans. She pulled them down and then pushed him back onto their bed.

"Lizzie, come on."

"It's okay. I just want to hold you. Touch you. You don't have to prove anything to me, John Daly. Just be with me. I'll take care of both of us."

And with that she pulled off her blouse, kicked off her pants, and unsnapped John's shirt. Leaning over him, she bent down and ran her tongue from his neck, down his chest, over his stomach and to his limp penis. She licked her finger and inserted it deep into her vagina and began massaging her clitoris. Meanwhile, she took him into her mouth and began sucking, imagining in her mind that the penis in her mouth was really a nipple, a huge, succulent nipple. Julia's nipple. The image of Julia's breast in her mouth made her hot and she could feel her body tingle as her finger found its mark and began a vibrating massage that brought Lizzie to a climax in less than a minute.

John, however, had remained flaccid and turned on his side, away from his wife, ashamed that he could not share in this most intimate of moments between two people. Soon the feelings of shame were replaced by rage over the intrusion into their lives by someone he once considered his friend. As he lay there, John contemplated various acts of revenge and reprisal. Justice would be done. For a brief moment, the thought of beating Paul to a pulp actually made John's penis hard, but as soon as Lizzie felt the bulge against her back, and she reached out to bring him inside her, the erection disappeared.

22

JULIA SAT ALONE in her bedroom, staring into a mirror attached to a large white dresser. She studied her reflection, searching her face for tell-tale signs of guilt, any noticeable clues to the turmoil she felt inside. How had everything gotten so out of hand? She should have told Lizzie about finding the car empty. Now this enraged stranger was out there stalking her best friend. Despite her anger over the situation Lizzie had put them in, Julia decided she had to warn her. But how could she do this without provoking her friend's wrath? It never took much to spark Lizzie's rage. It was if she kept a reserve of fury simmering just beneath the surface, ready to explode at any time. Julia had seen enough eruptions throughout their friendship to know the depth of ferocity she was likely to face. It sent a tremor down her back. Her mind was locked on this dilemma when Paul reached out to touch her shoulder.

"Agghh!" she screamed, jumping up.

"Honey?"

"I didn't hear you come in," she said, letting out a deep sigh.

"I'm sorry. I didn't mean to scare you."

Julia turned toward her husband and put her arms around him. "Just hold me." Paul wrapped his arms against her and she pressed herself into him. "I'm scared."

"Hey, I'm the one who screwed up. Let me take care of it."

"We should have told her."

"We will. I'm gonna tell them it was all my idea not to tell them about the body not being in the car and that I refused to let you say anything. Let her take it out on me. She hates me anyway."

"We're gonna face her together."

"I ain't been much of a husband, have I?"

Julia looked up at Paul's face. She felt a sadness bubble in her throat. "What are you talking about?"

"I let you down. All you ever wanted was to have a house full of kids and I haven't been able to give you even one. I can't even pay all the bills on my salary so you *have* to work."

"I like to work."

"You wanted to go to dental school. You should be filling teeth, not just cleaning them."

"I can still go. What about you? You had dreams. You were going to finish college and start your own company."

"It's like we just woke up one day and we were ten years older."

"It's not too late," she said, leaning her head against his chest. "We're still young."

"I should never have called her," said Paul, his head lowered. "I was just so mad at what she made us do."

"I know. We'll go over there later and straighten the whole mess out."

"Yeah. I'll grovel a bit. Let John hit me a couple times. They're our friends, right? Ya gotta stick by your friends."

Julia gave Paul a squeeze, and began to feel herself getting warm against his body.

"I was about to take a shower," she said, smiling. "Wanta join me?

"Why don't you go get started. I'm starving. I'm gonna make a sandwich."

"Make me one, too. Turkey with lots of mayo." She turned her head up and licked his jaw, then kissed him on the lips before heading for the bathroom, smiling over her shoulder as she left.

Paul blew out some air and sat up. Feeling empowered, he walked to the kitchen to begin the sandwiches.

Julia closed the door to the bathroom and turned on the shower. It usually took a few seconds to heat up. So she used the time to look in the mirror. Her cheeks were flush with sexual anticipation. There was a glow on her smooth face. Worry lines that had crossed her forehead before were beginning to fade along with the hardness around her eyes. She could feel her excitement grow as she stepped into the shower and let the hot pinprick spray awaken and arouse the more sensitive zones of her naked body. Everything was going to be all right, she thought as she poured some bath and shower gel into her right hand and began massaging her breast and between her thighs.

Paul opened the refrigerator and took out cellophane packages of sliced turkey and roast beef. He grabbed the mayonnaise bottle and a head of lettuce and put them on a counter next to the sink. He then pulled open the bread drawer and lifted out a fresh loaf of seven-grain bread. He could hear the shower running as he tore open the cellophane around the bread. As he fiddled with the bread wrapper, first trying to tear it open with his fingers, then giving up to use a knife, he thought he heard a scraping sound. But he wasn't sure where it came from. Must be one of the limbs on the two trees in front. He'd been meaning to cut them back from the house since he first noticed them pushing against the outside, but just hadn't gotten around to it. He'd better do something soon, or he'd be looking at a new paint job on the front of the house.

He returned to the refrigerator and took out a long neck bottle of beer, freshly made by a microbrewery next to the Ostrich. Paul opened the bottle and took a deep drink. He was tipping the bottle to his lips for a second swig when he heard the sound of breaking glass. He put the bottle down and walked toward the living room.

Julia let the pulsating water splash against her back and shoulders. The throbbing water massage felt like hot pinpricks and turned her skin pink. She arched her back to let the soothing spray smooth out the remnants of tension. She thought about her husband as she started to get aroused. She let her hand move between her legs and responded instantly to her own touch. Maybe she should wait until she was with Paul. But this felt too good to stop. With the hot water ramming down on her buttocks, she brought herself to a climax. She'd be ready again by the time Paul finished his sandwich.

Paul looked down at the broken glass on the floor next to the front door. He then saw the hole in the narrow row of windows that ran along each side of the door. "What the hell." He unlocked the front door and pulled it open.

The first shot knocked Paul back into the foyer. He looked down at his chest and saw blood bubbling through the hole in his right lung. The second shot hit him in the forehead, knocking his head back against the wall.

Julia rinsed the soap off her body and then turned off the water. She felt her way through the steam to a towel rack just outside the shower stall.

She wrapped one towel around her head and another around her body as she opened the door to the bathroom, letting a large cloud of steam out behind her. "Paul?"

She continued drying herself off in the bedroom, then put on her white terry-cloth bathrobe and walked toward the kitchen.

"Honey? What are you doing?"

Julia walked down the hallway to the kitchen. She saw the turkey, roast beef, mayonnaise and bread on the counter.

"Paul. Where'd you go?"

As soon as she entered the living room, she saw the breeze blowing the lace curtains over the windows next to the front door. "What happened here?" she said as she walked toward the foyer, nearly tripping over Paul's outstretched legs. It looked like he was sitting on the floor with his back against the wall.

"What are you...." But the words caught in her throat as she saw the bullet hole above his left eye and the chest wound that had stopped bubbling when Paul had stopped breathing.

"Oh, no," she cried, kneeling down next to him.

Julia put her fingers to his neck, praying for a pulse she knew would not be there. "Oh, Paul."

Suddenly, the fear took hold and she stood up, backing away from the front door. "Oh God." He must be out there. She ran into the bedroom and locked the door. She picked up the phone and began punching in 911.

"You have reached the emergency response number. State your emergency."

"Please. My husband's been shot. Four-twenty six Delaney Street. Hurry."

Julia hung up the phone and sat on her bed. He's found us. It's over. Everything is over.

23

THE POLICE CAR pulled into the driveway, passing within four feet of the person hiding in the shadows behind the wide maple tree that branched out over Julia's front yard. Neither of the two uniformed officers was aware of the presence in the darkness as they got out of the patrol car and walked toward the front door. Had they listened closely, they might have heard the hiss from a deep intake of breath that blended with other sounds of the night.

Bruce pressed himself into the bark of the tree and pondered the recklessness that had prevented him from fleeing into the night. A recurring thought flashed again, that he was here because he wanted to be caught, and then

150

punished. Why else would he take such a chance? He heard a doorbell ring from inside the house, and then the sound of a door opening. Should he look? He wanted to see her. But what if she saw him? It would be over. Maybe he should just turn himself in. He wasn't ready to do that yet. Instead he listened and heard her voice.

"He's over here," said Julia, still in a state of shock. She stood aside to let the police officers enter the foyer. The second officer pulled the door closed behind him.

Inside the house, Officer Daniel Larson bent down next to the body on the floor and checked for a pulse. Julia stood nearby leaning against the wall, holding herself against the chilling shivers that rippled up and down her back.

She watched the young officer take out a notebook and began noting the position of the body, the blood pool that had formed on the hardwood floor beginning under the body and then outward in a deep red oval. Julia estimated that Officer Larson was in his late 20s or early 30s. While he examined the body the second policeman, Officer Howard Curtis seemed to be studying the room, looking for something, on the walls, ceiling and floor. Curtis appeared to be in his early 20s.

Officer Larson stood up and sighed. "Anything?"

Officer Curtis shook his head "no."

"Keep looking," said Officer Larson. "I'll call it in."

"Do you want to use the phone?" asked Julia.

"That's okay," said Larson. "I'll use the car phone. Did you witness the shooting?"

"No. I was in the shower."

"Howie, I'm just gonna call in the homicide team and tell them to notify the M.E. Keep looking for the slug. It's gotta be here somewhere."

Larson went back outside while Officer Curtis began looking in the living room.

"Maybe it's still in him," offered Julia.

Officer Curtis kept searching as if he hadn't heard her.

Julia followed him into the living room. She watched as he bent down to examine a tear in the wallpaper.

"That's been there a while," said Julia. "Paul always said he was going to fix it but he never ..." She bowed her head and tears filled her eyes.

Officer Curtis sighed and continued his search. He stopped and turned back toward the foyer, estimating with his eyes any number of possible trajectories. He then began looking at the wall again, starting near the floor and then up to the ceiling.

Officer Larson returned and entered the living room. Julia wiped her eyes and tried not to keep staring at her husband's body.

"Can I ask you a question?" said Julia as Officer Larson joined his partner examining Paul's body.

"Sure ma'am," said Officer Larson.

"Why didn't you just use that phone over there?" asked Julia, pointing toward a black hand-held model sitting on an end table.

"Well, as of now, this room and the foyer are considered part of a crime scene. We'd prefer that you not touch or use anything in it. Also, the phone might contain information pertaining to this shooting, such as last number called, that sort of thing."

"I can tell you what the last number called was," said Julia. "It was you guys."

"In any event, ma'am, maybe you should follow me to another area of the house. There'll be a detective here shortly and he'll want to talk to you. I may have some questions as well. But right now it's imperative for my partner and I to find the kill shot."

"What makes you think it's not still in Paul?"

"There was an exit wound, ma'am. There's a slug in this room somewhere. Unless we find a broken window, then it could be a bit more difficult. But for any eventual prosecution purposes, it would help if we find the bullet that killed your husband. So if you'll just wait in here."

They were in the kitchen and Julia thought she was going to faint when she saw the half-made sandwich on the counter. The man who felt so incomplete in life had died with his last act unfinished.

A wave of cold rippled through Julia's body and she knew that she was going into shock. She quickly turned on the faucet and filled a plastic cup with water. She drank this down quickly to counter the burning bile that had been rising up in her chest. Warmth. Blankets. Where are the extra blankets? She left the kitchen and went to a hall closet where she found a small quilt. She wrapped the quilt around her shoulders and shivered. Goose bumps began to pop up all over her arms as she returned to the living room.

The enormity of what lay ahead brought with it an exhaustion that pushed Julia down onto a chair. She folded her arms on the kitchen table in front of her and then lowered her head onto her arms like she used to do in kindergarten when it was naptime. She'd give anything to turn back the clock to those days of innocence and joy. Closing her eyes, she tried to rewind the images stored in her memory. Anything to keep her mind off the future and the horror that lay ahead.

Unfortunately, the remembrance that replayed itself on the movie screen of her mind was of the time when she spent a night in jail. She was in eighth grade and hadn't met Lizzie yet. Even then, she picked the wrong friends. In this case, it was a tough group of girls from the poorest section of Lakeside known as the projects. It was where ninety percent of the town's crimes occurred. Julia's parents had forbidden her from ever going there, so of course, that's where her new friends would live.

There were three of them and they had next to nothing compared to all the other kids in Julia's class. They slept in living rooms of rundown apartments on torn sofas or mattresses on the floor with their siblings.

At least Julia's parents had their own home, even if it was tiny and furnished with tag sale mix-matched items. While her parents were far from wealthy, they made sure Julia had dinner whenever she was home. Two of her three friends in the projects didn't even know who their fathers were. Their mothers worked in factories or cleaned homes in the better sections of town. Julia's father worked at the post office and her mother had a part-time job at the A&P as a checkout person. That was then. Now, with her father retired, they lived in California north of Los Angeles near Julia's sister who was married to a drummer who worked for a movie score composer.

Julia had been left home alone the weekend she got into trouble. At 13, her parents thought she was responsible enough to be on her own. Her younger sister was spending the night on a sleepover with her best friend and her parents were in New Haven for a night of dining and dancing with a group of friends.

Around six, the girls from the projects stopped by. They were going to take the bus downtown and hang out at the mall.

"Don't the stores close at six?" asked Julia.

"Not on Saturdays. They're open till seven," answered Brenda, the unofficial leader of the group. "There's a lot to do. But we gotta hurry. The bus like takes forever."

When they finally arrived at the mall, many of the larger stores were just closing, so the girls entered a small boutique that catered to the upscale, but trendy crowd. Julia began to look at the new line of skirts when the other girls moved to the rear of the store and formed a circle around Brenda. Julia walked down the aisle to see what they were up to when she saw Brenda inside the circle trying to remove a plastic anti-theft device from the inside of a leather jacket.

"What are you doing?" demanded Julia.

"Shopping," snapped Brenda. "Keep your eye on that bitch up front."

Julia looked at the front of the store and saw an elderly woman watching them from behind the cash register.

"She's looking this way," said Julia.

"So go talk to her," said Brenda, still struggling with the plastic thing that looked like a fat clothespin. Giving up, Brenda took out a knife and cut the fabric around the plastic lock and eventually removed the device. She then put the leather jacket in a tote bag.

"Come on," said Brenda. "Let's get outta here. Take this will ya?" she said handing the tote to Julia. "It's okay. See. I took off the plastic thing."

"So why don't you carry the bag?" asked Julia.

"Because I been caught too many times and they'll want to see my bag," said Brenda. "But you, with that pretty, angel face will have no problem just walking out like the honest little honey you are baby."

The other girls winked as they started out the store. The woman behind the cash register looked at each one carefully, examining them with her eyes, seeing if they somehow managed to hide some piece of clothing. She didn't even give Julia a second glance as Julia began to leave the store. But as soon as Julia passed through the entrance, a loud blaring alarm went off. Julia froze. She stepped back into the store and the alarm stopped.

"Please come here, Miss," said the cashier.

Julia began to tremble as she walked over to the woman.

A security man appeared in the doorway and joined Julia and the woman at the cash register.

"I'll want to look in your bag," said the security guard.

"It's not my bag," stammered Julia, putting the tote on the counter.

The cashier reached in and pulled out the leather jacket. "What's this?" she said.

"I don't know," said Julia, now on the verge of tears. Meanwhile, Brenda and the other girls had scattered as soon as they heard the alarm.

"Someone's torn out one of our anti-shoplifting locks," said the cashier, "but she missed the other one we put in down here in the sleeve. You're in a lot of trouble, young lady."

Julia didn't know how to locate her parents. These were the days before cell phones. So she was told she was going to have to spend the night in jail until someone could come get her. She felt so ashamed as two police officers led her out of the mall and into the back of a patrol car. Brenda and the others watched from across the street and Brenda gave her a nod that indicated she knew Julia had not told the police the truth.

At the police station, the desk sergeant wanted the officers to take Julia home, but when he learned her parents were out of town, he reluctantly assigned her to a cell. The filth and smell were overwhelming. Julia was led to a large cell containing ten women, all twenty or more years older than she was. She imagined they were what Brenda would probably look like in a couple of decades if she didn't change her ways. Nearly all of the women smoked and smelled of sour sweat. A couple of them teased her and pretended to come on to her. The night dragged on forever, and Julia stayed awake out of fear that one of the women would kill her if she went to sleep. The next morning, Julia's parents signed the necessary papers and took their daughter home. She told them the story and they told her to either find a new group of friends or consider herself grounded until the end of school. It was shortly after that, when Julia met Lizzie.

24

JOHN DALY was watching Trailblazer pummel Texas Pete in an untitled grudge match on one of the numerous professional wrestling programs that occupied several cable franchises during prime time. John was a long time fan of the IWL, or the International Wrestling League, partly due to the fact that the headquarters for the IWL was in nearby Wilton. Lizzie hated wrestling and refused to let John even watch it when she was home so it was with mild disappointment that John greeted Lizzie's return from the store.

Trailblazer was just about to pin Texas Pete when Lizzie strode into the living room and shut off the television.

"Come on," whined John. "It's almost over."

"I'm starving. I want to eat," said Lizzie.

"Aw, man. Two more minutes."

"I picked up some Colonel Sanders," said Lizzie, walking to the kitchen. "If you hurry there might be some left."

John turned the TV back on but the match was over. He couldn't tell who won. He shut off the set and followed Lizzie into the kitchen.

"Hey," said John, dumping some fried chicken out onto a paper plate. "I think I figured it out."

Lizzie poured some iced tea into a glass and sat down before her plate, which was stacked high with a chicken breast, a leg and a wing, along with some mashed potatoes and a half ear of corn. "Figured what out?"

"You know, all the shit. I think it was Eddie the Hand. Think about it."

"Eddie the Hand?"

"Would Paul have the balls to do something like that? Never."

"He sure had the balls to blackmail us. I heard his voice."

"I can see him trying that. But not this other stuff."

"Why would Eddie the Hand do this?"

"That's what I wondered, too. Then it hit me. It's gotta be the ring."

"The ring?"

"You showed it to him, right? Maybe it really is worth a lot of money."

"We already know that."

"So, maybe he's mad that you took it back."

"I know he's mad. But he wouldn't set our Jeep on fire, or trash our house. He'd just come out and say, 'Give me the ring.' That's if he wanted it bad enough. I think something scared him off."

"What?"

158

"I don't know. All I know is that he didn't try very hard to keep it."

"Aw Lizzie, we're fucked, aren't we? You gotta get rid of that ring. Maybe this guy was one of those dudes from Bridgeport. The guys we now owe the money to. That's gotta be it. You showed the ring to Eddie. He either recognized it or told somebody about it who knew whose ring it was and those are the guys who are busting our chops right now. You gotta talk to Eddie. Find out how we can stop this shit. Make it right. Do whatever it takes, know what I'm saying?"

"I got a better idea," said Lizzie. "Why don't you go suck his cock this time?"

25

BRUCE WAS WRESTLING with whether or not to ring Julia's doorbell when an unmarked police car pulled up to the curb in front of her house. A plainclothes detective in his 40s got out of the car and walked across the lawn to the front door. Bruce caught a glimpse of the face in the street light. It was the face of a man who has seen too much sorrow in his lifetime. Would he show compassion if Bruce surrendered to him? His face said he might, but could Bruce be sure?

Julia heard the doorbell from the kitchen. Should she get up or let the officers who were still searching for a chunk of metal answer the door? On the second ring, Julia stood up and walked to the door. As she did, she looked into the foyer and living room and realized more people had arrived and were examining her house. Men and women in white lab coats were dusting and scraping. The third ring reminded Julia of her original destination and she opened the front door.

The man standing there wore a rumpled suit, of brown wool, a tie loosened at the neck and a police identification card in his wallet window.

"Detective Burger, ma'am. Are you Julia Stanton?"

"Yes."

"I'm sorry for your loss, Mrs. Stanton. May I come in?"

"Of course," said Julia, stepping aside so the detective could enter. Detective Harold Burger reminded Julia of that overweight detective on *NYPD Blue*. Andy Sipowicz? Was that his name? Detective Burger had the face of a retired prizefighter. His nose that had been flattened more than once and his cheekbones looked as if they had stopped a punch or two. He looked into the living room.

"I see our evidence team is already here," said Burger. "Do you mind if I have a word or two with my officers? Then I'd like to talk to you."

"Fine. I'll be in the kitchen." Julia watched Burger move into the foyer where Paul's body lay, unmoved since she found him there hours ago. It felt like a year had passed. Julia watched Burger kneel down to examine the body. Officer Larson pointed out the exit wound and nodded toward the living room where other officers had joined in the search for the missing slug.

Detective Burger looked up and saw Julia staring at him. He turned back toward Larson. "Have we checked the outside for footprints?"

"Not yet, sir. The evidence unit is still lifting fibers from the foyer."

"It looks like rain coming. You might want to pull off a couple of fibers and get some plaster of any tracks."

"Yes, sir."

Burger looked around and then rejoined Julia in the doorway.

"Why don't we sit down in there, Mrs. Stanton. I'm going to have to ask you a few questions."

"Of course."

She led him into the kitchen and sat down at the table. He took a chair across the table from her.

"I understand you were in the shower when the shooting occurred. Did you hear anything? Anyone talking?"

"No."

"Can you think of anyone who might have done this?

Julia's brow wrinkled briefly as if giving its own response, but then she faced the detective. "No."

"Were you and your husband having any problems?"

"What do you mean?"

"Marital problems."

"No. Not really."

"Not really what Mrs. Stanton?"

"Nothing all married couples don't go through. We'd fight over things. Argue. Not fight. Over money, mostly. We wanted children, but ... Well. It wasn't happening."

"What wasn't happening?"

"Conception. We tried everything. But it looked like the Good Lord just didn't want us to have children. Probably just as well cause we couldn't really afford any."

"Any other kind of problems?"

"Like what?"

"Do you or your husband own any firearms?"

"No."

"Are any valuables missing?"

"Valuables? Ah. I don't know. I haven't looked."

"Could you do that now, please?"

"Sure." Julia looked around the kitchen. She opened some drawers. She left the kitchen and walked down a hallway to a bedroom. Detective Burger followed behind. In the bedroom, she walked over to a dresser and opened a small wooden box. She sifted through the jewelry in the box and then closed the lid.

"I don't think anything's missing."

"Were you or your husband seeing anyone?"

"Seeing anyone?"

"Having an affair?"

"No."

"What kind of insurance policy did your husband have?"

"Insurance? Life insurance?"

"Yes."

"I don't know. Why?"

"Just a routine question, ma'am."

"Routine? Somebody breaks into my house while I'm taking a shower, shoots my husband twice and leaves. Is that routine?"

"Maybe we should continue this discussion at the police station."

"Police station. Why?"

"I think you know something."

"I do not know who killed my husband."

"I want you to take a lie detector test."

"You don't believe me?"

"No ma'am, I don't."

"A lie detector test. Do I have to?"

"No. But if you refuse, your refusal will be recorded. Plus, I'll never believe another thing you tell me. Also, if you don't take the test, I would recommend that you call your lawyer."

"I don't have a lawyer."

"We would arrange for you to retain one."

"I don't need a lawyer."

"Then you should have no problem with the test."

"I'm just not good with tests. What if I tell the truth and it thinks I'm lying? I know how I am. I feel guilty sometimes when I'm not. You know if someone says 'hey my wallet's been stolen,' my first thought is that they're going to think I took it even when I didn't."

"We have ways to get past that sort of thing."

"I don't have much choice then, do I?"

"Actually, you do. You can refuse, and we'd have to make note of that, but then your refusal might cast suspicion, if you know what I mean."

"Suspicion. On me, you mean."

"Well, that's one way to look at it. It's been our experience that most homicides are committed by someone close to the victim."

"I'll take the test," said Julia.

26

LIZZIE COULD HEAR the shouts of announcers and fans banging through the wall of her bedroom. John had returned to his wrestling. She opened a drawer in the end table next to her side of the bed and took out a piece of paper with an address written on it. She then took out the ring and looked it over. Who were you? "Salesman of the Year." What were you selling?

John was gnawing on a chicken leg watching the main event when Lizzie entered the living room.

"Just one more match."

"I'm going back out for awhile."

"Now where are you goin?"

"We're outta beer. I'll just run down to the Seven-eleven."

"Pick me up some nacho chips. Barbecue flavor. The big bag."

Lizzie stepped out into the night and closed the door behind her. She banged her knee climbing into the compact two-door rental car they had until they could scrape together enough money to buy a larger piece of junk. She pulled out of the driveway and drove away slowly, checking the address on the piece of paper from the bedroom.

It took about ten minutes to find the street she was looking for. It was a commercial street of closed storefronts. A muffler shop, next to a place that sold beepers and cell phones, next to a body shop, and a car wash. All the stores were deserted at this time of night.

She stopped next to a warehouse with the words "Tire Barn" stenciled on the outside. She turned off the engine and got out of the car, once again checking the address on the paper.

There was a light on the second floor of the warehouse. She found a door which apparently led to where the light was coming from and knocked.

"It's open," came a voice from inside.

Lizzie opened the door and stepped inside. There was a long flight of stairs just inside the door. "Up here."

Lizzie began walking up the stairs.

Eddie the Hand was sitting on a gray metal desk, cleaning his fingernails with a knife when Lizzie appeared in the doorway of a small office.

"You're late."

"I've had a tough day. Did you tell anybody about this ring?"

"What if I did?"

"Did you?"

"Fuck no. Who would I tell?"

Lizzie held her hand open and Eddie reached out and lifted it from her palm. He smiled and then leaned down to open a drawer of the desk.

"That was seven, right?"

"It's worth a lot more than that and you know it."

Eddie counted out seven 100-dollar bills.

"So take it somewhere else. You might be able to get more for it, along with a ration of shit from the police when whoever you sell it to tries to get it valued at one of those fancy jewelry stores on Summit Street. It's up to you cupcake. Seven's my final offer. Unless, like I said, you got the 35-thousand you owe. Then I said I'd give you eight. You got the 35? No?"

He held the money out and Lizzie took it and stuffed it in her purse.

"What? No thanks?"

"Thanks," she said, turned, shut her purse and walked out of the office. Eddie looked at the ring and raised his eyebrows. He got out an eyepiece, the kind jewelers use, and examined the diamonds embedded in the gold. He heard the door open and close down at the bottom of the stairs. He waited a few more seconds until he heard a car engine start, then picked up the phone and punched in a number. Someone answered on the first ring.

"Hey," said Eddie. "I just got something you might be interested in. A real beauty. Makes that thing you're wearing look like a rat turd. For you, two thousand. Believe me, it's worth more than twice that. Come by the office in the morning."

Eddie hung up the phone and stood up from the desk. He turned off the desk lamp and was heading for the door when he heard a creak in the hallway at the top of the stairs.

"Who's there?"

Slowly, Eddie reached for another drawer. He pulled it open and saw the magnum nine-millimeter lying on top of a *Hustler* magazine.

It was the last thing he saw as the shot caught him behind the ear. The bullet exited through the left temple of Eddie's forehead, taking a half-dollar sized chunk of skull with it.

Eddie the Hand fell across the desk, still clutching the ring. A gloved hand reached down and pried his fingers open and removed the ring. Another hand opened the drawer on the desk where Eddie kept his money and found several stacks of hundred dollar bills. The hand removed the money and closed the drawer.

27

JULIA HAD NOT BEEN inside the Lakeside Police station since that fateful night in junior high school. The building had been completely remodeled over the years so nothing was familiar to her when she entered the lobby. She recalled there had been lots of bars and cells but these apparently had been replaced with rooms to interrogate suspects and workstations for the officers. The new lobby reminded her of a doctor or dentist's office. There were plastic chairs along the wall for people to sit in while they waited for whatever business had brought them to this place. Detective Burger nodded to the person behind a glass window, who then apparently hit a switch that unlocked the door to the right of the window.

"Follow me, Mrs. Stanton," commanded Detective Burger as he opened the door and held it for her.

Behind the door, there was a large open room with workstations being manned by people in and out of uniforms. Detective Burger began walking toward the rear of the room. Julia started to follow him when she passed a computer screen on one of the workstations and stopped.

Detective Burger noticed she had stopped and went to find out why. On the screen of the computer was a photograph of Bruce.

"You know him?"

The question startled Julia, who immediately turned away from the computer.

"Huh?"

"The photo. It looked like you recognized the person on the computer."

"Oh, no. I ... He looked familiar, that's all."

"The police from Huntington, Long Island are after him."

"What did he do?"

"I'm not sure. It's not my case. Something about a dead wife."

Julia felt as if someone had punched the breath out of her.

"We're just going back there." Detective Burger nodded toward an office in the rear of the station. But Julia was staring at the photo of Bruce again. Detective Burger took her by the arm and began to lead her to the rear of the large room. As they walked, Julia glanced back toward the picture of Bruce one more time and then looked ahead. She realized Detective Burger was staring at her so she smiled at him. "He looks so much like a cousin of mine. It's amazing."

They eventually came to a closet-sized office that contained a machine that looked like a hospital EKG monitor. Two plainclothes officers were in the office when Julia and Detective Burger entered.

"This is Officer Mark Treat," said Detective Burger. He'll be conducting the polygraph test."

Julia shook the young officer's hand. He had delicate women's hands and was extremely thin. Julia wondered if he was ill.

"And this is Officer Emily Douglas." Julia turned to the woman standing along the wall. She nodded unsmiling at Julia. "I've asked Officer Douglas to be present," said Detective Burger. "Procedure."

Julia forced a smile as she looked from one to the other. They did not return her smile.

"Please sit down," said Officer Treat.

Julia took the chair next to the polygraph machine. As soon as she was seated, Officer Treat began to attach electrodes to predetermined points on Julia's body. Her wrist, upper shoulder, back of her neck, her ankle, inner arm.

"You won't be able to feel anything," explained Officer Treat. "The machine will read various body signals. The polygraph test consists of three parts. The pneumograph records your respiration, the depth and rate of your breathing. The galvanograph monitors any changes in your skin, and the cardiograph registers any variations in your blood pressure or pulse rate."

"And I'm not going feel anything?"

"No. Just relax, sit back and answer the questions as honestly as possible. Don't stress yourself or try to control your responses. That could throw off the test. Are you ready?"

"I guess so. How accurate is this?"

"Ninety-eight percent. I'm gonna ask you questions that you should answer with only a simple 'yes' or 'no.' If you don't understand a question, simply remain silent or raise your hand. Okay?"

171

"I guess."

"For starters, I need to determine your normal response level. I'll do that by asking you a few meaningless questions. Just answer 'yes' or 'no' and answer honestly. Okay?"

"Okay."

"Is today Thursday?"

"No."

Officer Treat held up a play card, the three of clubs.

"Is this the three of clubs?"

"Yes."

"Is George Washington the President?"

"No."

"Are the colors of the American flag red, white and blue?"

"Yes."

Officer Treat consulted a file, then looked up.

"Are you thirty-three-years old."

"No."

"Now, I want you to lie. Pick a card."

Julia picked a playing card from a deck lying on a table next to the chair.

"Don't tell me what it is. I will tell *you* from your responses. You are to answer 'no' to my questions about the card, even if I say the right card. Okay?

"I guess."

She looked at the card. It was the nine of diamonds.

"Put it back in the deck."

She did, and he picked up the deck and searched for the card she looked at. He picked out a card.

"Is it the eight of hearts?"

"No."

Then another.

"Is it the four of clubs?"

"No."

"The seven of clubs?"

"No."

"Is it the nine of diamonds?"

"No."

He looked at the machine and then at Julia. "It was the nine of diamonds."

"How did you know?"

"Look." Officer Treat nodded at the needles on the polygraph machine. Julia looked at the lines on graph paper and saw the spike where he had asked about the nine of diamonds.

"Amazing."

"Did you kill your husband?" asked Officer Treat.

The question startled Julia, who looked at the policeman.

"No!"

"Were you and your husband having marital problems?"

"No."

"Do you know who may have killed your husband?"

"No."

"Did you hire someone to shoot your husband?"

"No."

"Do you know of anyone who was angry at your husband?"

"No."

Officer Treat marked the test paper.

"Are you afraid for your own life?"

"Yes. I mean No."

Officer Treat made another notation.

"Are you withholding any information that could relate to your husband's shooting?"

"No."

Officer Treat looked at the test and then at Julia.

"Okay. I think we're finished. Officer Douglas will take you back to Detective Burger. I'll try to have the results as soon as possible."

Officer Douglas removed the wires and discs from Julia's arms and ankles. She helped her stand up and led her out of the room as Detective Burger entered from another entrance.

"Did she shoot her husband?"

"Not according to this. But she might know who did."

"Might?"

"Nothing conclusive, here, mind you. This is not an exact science, but I'd say she knows a heck of a lot more than she's telling us. There's something else."

"What else?"

"I would say that she's obviously afraid that whoever killed her husband may try to kill her, too."

28

JULIA WAS SITTING on the plastic chairs in the station lobby when Detective Burger found her. He was with Officer Larson, one of the first patrolmen to arrive on the scene.

"Mrs. Stanton. I'm going to have Officer Larson drive you home."

"That's it? You're not even going to tell me how I did?"

"The test was inconclusive."

"What's that supposed to mean? Do you really think I killed my husband?"

"No, ma'am. I don't."

"So what's the problem?"

"I think you're withholding evidence."

"Evidence? I don't have any evidence."

"Knowledge, then. You may want to retain an attorney, Mrs. Stanton."

"But I don't know anything, either."

"I'll be in touch. Meanwhile, take my card, in case you think of something that might bear on your husband's shooting. Just remember, withholding information could lead to an obstruction of justice charge."

Detective Burger handed her his business card, which she looked at, and then looked up at Detective Burger. There were tears in her eyes.

"I didn't kill my husband. I don't know who did. Please believe me."

"Goodnight, Mrs. Stanton. And just one more thing. Check with me before going out-of-town."

Julia tried to respond but Burger was already walking through the door that led to the large office behind the wall and the window cage. Officer Larson cleared his throat. "Is there some place you'd like to stay tonight. A relative? A friend?"

"Just take me home," said Julia, who let out a sigh and walked out the front door of the police station.

Twenty minutes later, they were sitting in the patrol car in Julia's driveway. Officer Larson put the car in park and waited for Julia to get out. When she didn't move, he turned toward her.

"Are you sure you wanta stay here tonight, Mrs. Stanton?"

"Huh?"

"It might be better if you stayed with a friend or relative. That's all I'm saying. Is there anyone nearby?"

"No. My parents live in California. I just want to go home."

"Well, then, we're here."

"We are?" Julia looked at her house as if it had appeared by magic. "Oh, okay. Thanks."

She was about to get out of the car when Officer Larson said, "Just remember that parts of your house might still be off limits. The foyer and living room."

"How am I going to get in, then?"

"You'll have to go in through the garage."

"How long do I have to put up with this?"

"Just until crime scene gives us the clear signal. Shouldn't be much longer. They still haven't found the slug."

"I'm sorry. I don't mean to take it out on you."

"That's okay." Officer Larson looked embarrassed.

"Thanks for the ride."

Julia started to get out of the car when Officer Larson turned off the engine and got out his side as well.

"I'll be okay."

"I just remembered that I was told to check your house, ma'am."

"Fine."

Julia and Officer Larson entered through the garage door into the laundry room and then the kitchen. Larson immediately began searching rooms and closets. Julia remained in the kitchen staring out at the yellow crime scene tape across the door to the foyer and living room. She then saw the blood on the floor. Without being able to control herself, Julia bowed her head and began to weep. She sat down at the kitchen table and sobbed into her hands.

"Oh, Paul."

A few minutes later, Officer Larson stood in the kitchen looking down at Julia. She realized his presence and raised her head, wiping her eyes.

"Mrs. Stanton. You sure you wouldn't be more comfortable at a motel or ..."

"I'll be okay."

"Right. I'll just ... Goodnight, Mrs. Stanton."

Officer Larson let himself out as Julia wiped more tears from her eyes.

She locked the door behind him and then walked to the bedroom. The room never seemed so empty. She looked at the bed and then at the photo of she and Paul on her dresser. She picked up the eight-by ten picture and frame and held it to her chest.

"What have we done? Who is this monster we've unleashed? First Lizzie and John's Jeep. Now Paul. This creep isn't going to stop until we're all dead. Why should he? A man who murders his own wife. What's so hard about killing a few strangers, especially ones who tried to kill him? Please God, I know I haven't been much of a praying person, but I'm begging you tonight. You're all I've got left. Are you gonna help me get through this? Or do I have to face it all on my own as usual? I have to warn Lizzie. If he found us, he'll be able to find her. Why didn't I just tell the police? It's all so confusing. I don't know what to do any more. You understand what I'm saying, God? A little direction. That's all I'm asking. What should I do? Is that too much to ask? Guess so."

Julia picked up her telephone. She had to call somebody. What was she going to tell her parents? Oh hi Mom, Dad. What's new? Me? Well, Paul got shot tonight. We think it might be this guy Lizzie met the other night who killed his wife. You see, Lizzie shot him and then we pushed his car into a lake. But somehow he survived so he's gonna kill us all now to set things right. How about you guys? How's California?

Maybe she should just call Lizzie. She was going to have to tell her sooner or later. Julia dreaded this call more than anything. But she'd better make it. What if this guy is already on his way over there? She had to warn her. Julia punched in Lizzie's number.

29

JOHN THREW his empty box of fried chicken at the television when Chicago Dave tripped the Surgeon just as the Surgeon was about to put Trailblazer to sleep with his special move. The trip gave Trailblazer just enough time to pin the Surgeon and win the match.

"Shit," snarled John as he got off the recliner and headed for the kitchen. As he stood up, the phone rang.

What the fuck, thought John. He wasn't expecting any calls. Besides, it was probably for Lizzie. Most calls were. It doesn't matter, thought John, because he didn't feel like talking to anyone. So he let the phone ring as he walked to the kitchen.

He opened the refrigerator and looked inside. "Jesus, where the hell did she go for beer, Hartford?"

He closed the refrigerator door and opened the freezer. There he found a frosted bottle of vodka. He took the bottle out and poured himself a glass in one of Brian's Star Wars glasses.

John was about to take a sip when Brian entered the kitchen rubbing his eyes and saw his father drinking from his glass.

"Hey," said Brian. "That's mine."

"Can't I use it?" asked John. "I'll wash it out when I'm done."

"I'm hungry," said Brian. "Make me some cereal."

"Cereal? It's bedtime. How come you're not in bed?"

"I was in bed, but I wet my pants."

"So put on some clean ones."

"I don't have any."

"Doesn't she do anything around here? Okay, I'll check the laundry room."

"Can I have some cereal first?"

"Oh, okay. But don't sit down if you're all full of pee. We don't want you stinking up the kitchen."

John took another drink and put the glass on top of the refrigerator so Brian couldn't reach it. He then took out some Captain Crunch and a bottle of one percent milk. He put the cereal and milk in a bowl and set it on the table with a spoon.

"Maybe you should take those wet pants off and I'll put them right in the washer. Then you should take a bath while the clothes are washing."

"A bath?"

"Yes, a bath. You're covered with pee. I can smell it all the way over here."

"But it's so late. Can't I eat my cereal first?"

"Fine. Eat your cereal and then it's bath time. I'll get the tub ready and then start the laundry."

Brian started eating while John took his vodka and went to the bathroom Brian used across from his bedroom. John let the water run until it started to get hot and then turned it down so it was lukewarm. He tested the water and then returned to the kitchen.

"Okay, the bath's all set. Just take your pants off and leave them on the floor."

Brian filled his mouth with milk and cereal and squiggled out of his wet pajama bottoms. "Where's Mommy?"

"She had to go out and get some groceries. She should be back soon."

"Did you put my GI Joes in the tub?"

"No. You're not gonna be in there that long. Just get clean and get back into bed."

"I want my toys."

"Brian. Okay. Where are they?"

"In the family room. I'll get them."

Brian ran off to get his toys leaving his soggy bottoms on the kitchen floor.

John took another drink and picked up the pajamas with two fingers and headed for the laundry room, carrying the urine soaked pjs in one hand and his glass of vodka in the other.

As soon as he got to the laundry room, he put down his glass and pushed the light switch. Only the light didn't come on. "Great. How am I supposed to do the laundry in the dark?"

John felt his way to the washer and opened the top. The washer was filled with damp clothes smelling of mildew. "Jesus, these smell worse than before they were washed."

John stuck the wet pajama bottoms on top of the clothes already in the washer and searched for detergent. He found a box of Tide but when he turned it upside down over the washer, nothing came out. The box was empty. "Shit." He looked around the darkened room and realized there were overflowing baskets of dirty laundry everywhere.

"She go on a laundry strike, or what."

John opened a cabinet and found some Stay Fresh fabric softener and a bottle of bleach. "This will have to do." He poured some of the fabric softener onto the damp clothes and then turned on the water. While the washer filled, he poured in some of the bleach, splashing some of the clear liquid over the urine-drenched pajamas.

He then closed the lid on the washer and left the laundry room.

Brian was playing with his plastic soldiers when John looked in on him, splashing in the tub. "Hey, you got the floor all wet," said John.

"Sorry."

"Your pajamas are in the wash. They'll be ready by the time you finish your bath. I'm gonna watch some TV. Don't get water all over the place, okay?"

John returned to the kitchen and looked around for his glass. He then remembered he'd left it in the laundry room. Walking back into the darkened laundry room, he searched the counter behind the washer with his hand, feeling for the glass that contained his vodka. His fingers touched the round glass and he lifted it off the ledge, toasted the washer and brought the glass of clear liquid directly to his lips. He took a long drink, finishing off the glass.

The powerful burning sensation raked at his throat and he dropped the glass. "What the fuck?" he thought. He opened his mouth to take a breath but his throat had closed off involuntarily. He tried to breathe, but nothing was getting through. His chest was on fire and his esophagus burned like a pole on fire. Gasping for air that refused to penetrate his sealed throat, he staggered out of the laundry room and into the light of the hallway.

"My God," his mind screamed. "What's happening to me?"

John reached out to the wall with one hand while the other hand grabbed his neck. He pulled on his Adam's apple. His head felt like it was going to explode. He opened his mouth again and tried to speak, but nothing came out.

He tried to walk but fell to the floor as his stomach clenched in a cramp that made him double over in excruciating pain.

In his bathtub, Brian was playing with his toy soldiers when he heard the crash coming from hallway. He looked curiously. "Daddy?"

The first thing he saw was the hand, grabbing the door opening near the floor. Then he saw his father's face, grimaced in pain.

"You're scaring me, Daddy. Don't scare me."

John crawled along the floor, pushing himself into the opening of the bathroom door. His face and neck were dark red and his eyes were filled with tears. He tried again to speak but failed. He tried to pull himself into the bathroom and up to a sink but fell back to the floor. Water. He needed water. He had to put the fire out. Brian's bath. He started to crawl toward the tub. He found puddles of water on the bathroom floor and began to lick at them like a dog. Brian's eyes widened. He started to laugh. But then his father made a gasping, gurgling sound and his face turned deep purple. His neck cords were straining, about to burst. He raised his head off of the floor and moved toward the tub, his face inches from the cold ceramic top of the tub, just beyond which lay warm soapy bath water. He was about to push the final few inches into the water when a tremor wrenched him back to the bathroom floor, where he shuddered in a death rattle and stopped. Brian looked over the tub and down at his father lying still on the floor. John's eyes were wide open but unseeing.

Brian splashed some water out of the tub on to his father's face. But John didn't move.

A shadow fell across Brian and he looked up. His mother was looking down at him.

"I think it's time to get out of the tub, big guy," said Lizzie. "What's the matter with your father? He drunk again?"

Lizzie wrapped Brian in a towel and lifted him out of the bath. She turned, holding her son, and stepped over the prone body of her husband. Brian looked down at his father.

"You can get up now, Daddy. I'm all done."

"Hear that, honey? You can get up now. Let's let Daddy sleep, okay?"

Lizzie carried Brian down the hallway to his bedroom. "What were you and Daddy playing?"

"He was sneaking up on me, but I saw him."

"He's never been good at sneaking up."

"What's that smell?"

"What smell?"

"That funny, yucky smell."

Lizzie sniffed the air. "Why, that's bleach, honey. We use it to make your clothes nice and bright. Was Daddy doing some laundry?"

"I wet my bed."

"I see," said Lizzie, putting Brian down in the hallway. "Then we need new sheets." She got some clean bedding out of a closet. "How about your pj's?"

"Daddy was washing them."

"Here's some clean underwear. Put them on and we'll worry about pj's in the morning. I'm too tired to do any laundry tonight."

"How come Daddy isn't getting up?"

"Let me go see."

Lizzie returned to the bathroom and nudged John with her foot.

"Come on, John. Wake up. Stop foolin around now. It's late. We want to go to bed."

Lizzie knelt down next to him and pulled him over. "Okay, John, this isn't funny."

John's head turned toward Lizzie and she could see his lifeless eyes. "John?"

Brian came up behind his mother and looked over her shoulder.

"Is Daddy sick?" asked Brian.

"I think so," said Lizzie. "I better call the doctor.

Lizzie stood up. There were tears in her eyes. She picked up Brian and carried him back out of the bathroom. "Come on. Let's get you tucked in and then I'll call the doctor."

"Is Daddy going to be all right?"

"Sure. He probably had too much to drink."

It was about three a.m. when the EMS van arrived and the two-man crew tried to revive John Daly. They put his body on a stretcher and carried him to the van.

Lizzie followed the two men outside.

"We're going to have to record this as dead at the scene, ma'am. Maybe if we'd got here a little sooner, we might have been able to do something," said a man with the name Davenport stenciled on his shirt. "Do you have any idea why your husband would drink a glass of bleach?"

"I wasn't here. My son says he was doing the laundry. I found a glass of vodka next to the washer. He must have poured some bleach into a similar glass and got them mixed up."

"Ouch," said Davenport.

"Where are you taking him?"

"Morgue. Chances are they'll wanta do an autopsy."

"Why? Isn't it obvious how he died?"

"Policy. Coroner has to issue a ruling. Chances are it'll be accidental death by ingestion of chlorine bleach, but they gotta go through the motions."

Lizzie looked down at John's body as they carried him to the van. She watched them close the van doors, get in and drive off into the night. As soon as they were gone, Lizzie returned to her house, closed the door behind her, and let out a deep sigh.

She walked to the laundry room and removed the clothes from the washer and put them in the drier. She looked around the room, found some light bulbs and replaced the one in the socket. She turned on the light and left the room.

In the kitchen, Lizzie went to the grocery bag that she left on the table and pulled out a six pack of beer. She opened a bottle of St. Pauli Girl and took a healthy swig.

Julia was lying in bed staring up at the ceiling when the phone rang. She looked at the radio alarm clock and saw that it was 3:36 a.m. She looked at the phone as it continued to ring. Who would be calling at this hour? Could it be him? Checking to see if she's home, alone. What if it's the police? No. They would just show up. So would the Stranger. Slowly, she reached for the phone and lifted the receiver.

"Hello."

"Lizzie?"

"Julia. I'm sorry to call at this hour, but I didn't know who else to call. John's dead."

"What?" Julia sat up in her bed. "What happened? Oh, my God."

"The asshole drank some bleach. He confused it with a glass of vodka."

"Lizzie, I ..."

"I know. What can you say?"

"No. It's not that. I called you before but nobody answered. You're not going to believe this."

"What?"

"Paul was shot tonight!"

"Oh, shit. Is he all right?"

"No. He's dead."

"Paul's dead?"

"Oh, Lizzie, I should have told you. I'm sorry."

"Is this freaky, or what? I mean, what are the chances of something like this happening? Both our husbands die on the same night. What's going on here? Tell me about Paul. Who shot him?"

"I don't know. Well, I think I know, but ..."

"You do?"

"Lizzie, there's something I should have told you."

"What?"

"The man you picked up. He's alive."

"What are you talking about?"

"The man you shot. In the car. He's alive."

Lizzie dropped the phone from her hand. She picked the receiver back up.

"He can't be."

"He is, Lizzie. And he's coming to get us."

"Julia. You're imagining things."

"I'm coming over. We shouldn't be alone. I'll explain everything when I get there."

"Julia. Wait. How could he possibly be alive? I shot him in the head. You checked his pulse. He was dead. We pushed his car into the reservoir."

"I know. I'll explain it when I get there."

"Explain what!" shouted Lizzie. "What's to explain?"

30

LIZZIE FINISHED OFF her beer as she pondered what Julia had told her. She saw the car sink into the water of the reservoir. She replayed in her mind shooting the Stranger in the head. How could he possibly be alive? Julia must be hallucinating. Maybe she was having a nervous breakdown over everything. First the Stranger, Paul's murder and then John's death. Now Julia was coming over. Lizzie had to prepare.

She left the kitchen and went into Brian's bedroom. Her son was curled up on his bed on top of his covers, sound asleep. She nudged his shoulder.

"Brian. Wake up. You're going over to Grandma's tonight."

Bruce was switching through channels on the television in his hotel room when he saw Julia being led out of her house by the police. He quickly went back to the channel, which appeared to be a local cable access channel, for 24-hour local news. He turned up the sound and heard the anchor man say, "According to police, Mrs. Stanton told them she was taking a shower when the intruder broke into their home and shot her husband. Police are asking anyone with information about the shooting to call 555-3400. Meanwhile, the clean-up for Long Island Sound resumes tomorrow."

Bruce hit the mute button and picked up the photo he had taken from Lizzie's house. It was the one of Lizzie, Paul, John and Julia smiling and leaning into each other. He was staring at the photo when one of the faces in it appeared in a photo on television. Bruce hit the mute button again and the sound returned.

"In an apparent unrelated incident," said the anchor, "another Lakeside man died early this morning when he mistakenly drank a glass of bleach thinking it was vodka."

Bruce compared the photo in his hand to the one on the television screen. It was the man standing next to Lizzie in the photo.

"John Daly, a self-employed carpenter, lived at…"

Detective Roy McCarthy drove into the parking lot in the back of the Lakeside police station. His eyes were still red from sleep deprivation. He put his car in park, shut off the engine, got out and entered the building, feeling as if he were sleep walking.

Chief Manzini was waiting for him just inside the station with a cup of coffee in a Styrofoam cup.

"Black, no sugar," he said handing it to McCarthy.

"Do we have him?"

"Not exactly."

"But you said we may have found my man."

189

"'May' being the key word. Hey, if I'm wrong, shoot me. You wanted a call if anything came in."

"Okay."

"Come on. It might be nothin, who knows," said Manzini as he led the way back into the station main office. "We had a woman in here earlier. Her husband had been shot. While she was here, she saw the photo of your man, Wilson. It seemed to jolt her."

"Jolt her?"

"That's what I was told by the Detective who questioned her. He says that when he asked her about it, she pretended not to know him. Said he looked like her cousin."

"Why didn't he believe her?"

"Something in her face. Her expression."

"Expression?"

"For a brief moment, she looked terrified."

"You got an address on this woman?"

"I got something even better."

"You did find him."

"Maybe. One of our patrol units was canvassing hotels and motels. A clerk at this hotel just off I-95 said a man who checked in yesterday looked like our boy."

"Let's go."

"Take it easy. I sent a unit out. He's not there."

"Let's take a look at his room, then."

"We could do that. It really bothers me that this woman tagged your killer."

"Why?"

"We gave her a lie detector test and she seemed to be hiding something about her husband's murder. Maybe your boy was involved somehow."

"I was afraid of that."

Julia locked the door behind her as she stepped into her garage. She heard a scratching sound near the garbage cans that were filled and ready to be put outside first thing in the morning. She hit the switch on the wall to open the garage door. While the door opened, Julia walked to her car and was about to get inside when another sound grabbed her attention. She looked out the open garage door and saw some bushes moving. A blade of ice and fear made her freeze.

He's here, she thought. Slowly, she opened the door on the driver's side and began to lower herself behind the wheel when she heard the crash!

She slammed the door and locked it. She fumbled with the keys, dropping them on the floor. She bent down, searching with her fingers, anxious sweat spraying from her face. Movement. The garbage can was rolling toward the car.

Oh, God. Please, God. Her fingers found the keys. She sat up and jammed them in the ignition, and turned. Her foot pressed down the accelerator and she shifted into reverse.

The car surged from the garage, bouncing over the thick rubber garbage can, spewing garbage every where. But Julia didn't even look back. As soon as the car hit the street, she shifted into drive and burned rubber for half a block as she sped off into the night. She didn't even pause to close the garage door.

Had she looked back, she would have seen the raccoon emerge sheepishly from the bushes and enter the garage. The animal looked around quickly and then began tearing at the plastic bags that contained its first meal of the day.

31

DETECTIVE MCCARTHY and Chief Manzini were just about to leave the station when an officer stopped Manzini in the lobby and whispered something to him. Manzini nodded and then turned to McCarthy.

"I'm afraid I'm not going to be able to join you in your little search. We just got word of another shooting death."

"Two shootings and an accidental poisoning, all in one night. So much for the suburbs being the safe alternative to the big bad city," joked McCarthy.

"This latest one isn't much of a surprise. I'm just amazed this guy lived as long as he did, considering the shit he's pulled."

"Who's that?"

"This loan shark. Eddie the Hand was his street name. He's usually on the other end of this sort of thing. Nothing we could ever prosecute, but we knew he was responsible for about a half-dozen homicides in the last ten years. He was connected, so someone's probably going to pay."

"So what am I supposed to do about Wilson?" asked McCarthy.

Manzini was thinking about the question when Officer Larson returned from his rounds and was about to log off when the chief put his hand out.

"Officer Larson. I know you've had a busy night, but would you mind escorting Detective McCarthy from the Huntington, Long Island Police Department to the Evergreen Motel? Here's a warrant that allows Detective McCarthy to search a room registered to Bruce Wilson, not necessarily the name on the motel's card file, but it's who we believe has booked the room. Mr. Wilson is wanted in connection with the death of his wife."

"No problem, Chief. Evergreen Motel. Off I-95, near the train station."

"That's the one."

It was nearly four a.m. when Detective McCarthy and Officer Larson pulled up in front of the Evergreen Motel. If Wilson wasn't in his room, wondered Detective McCarthy, then where was he? What was his connection to this Stanton woman? An old flame, maybe? McCarthy hated to admit this was turning into a good old-fashioned mystery. And, unlike many in his profession, he just loved a good mystery. He just hoped his boy hadn't gone on a killing spree.

They retrieved a master key from the desk clerk who offered no resistance when they produced their badges. The door to each unit opened up onto the parking lot. McCarthy and Officer Larson were walking past the window to the room Bruce Wilson had been assigned when they heard voices coming from inside. They froze and listened. A man and woman were talking about a new pet store in Lakeside.

"I thought he was supposed to be out," whispered Detective McCarthy.

"I know that voice," whispered Larson. "The woman, anyway. She's on our local cable news channel."

"He must be watching television," replied McCarthy. "Are you ready?"

Larson nodded.

Detective McCarthy knocked on the door.

"Mr. Bruce Wilson. This is Detective McCarthy of the Huntington Police Department. Please open the door."

They waited and listened, but heard no sound other than the conversation on the television.

McCarthy knocked again.

"Mr. Wilson. We just want to talk to you. Please open the door."

Still no response. Detective McCarthy inserted the master key into the lock, turned it, and pushed the door open. He had his gun drawn and stepped through the door with the pistol held out in two hands in fire position.

Officer Larson followed him in, his gun also out and aimed in front. They looked around at the empty room. The television was on. Officer Larson quickly checked in the bathroom and closet.

"He's not here," said Larson.

Detective McCarthy put his gun away and bent down to pick up a photograph lying on the unmade bed. As he studied the picture, Larson looked over his shoulder at the same photo.

"Holy shit!" shouted Larson.

Detective McCarthy looked up at the patrolman. "I beg your pardon."

"That woman there, in the photo." He pointed at Julia. "That's Julia Stanton. It was her husband that was shot last night."

"The loan shark?"

"No. The other guy. I took the call."

"She must be the woman who recognized Wilson's photograph. You know where she lives?"

"I drove her home a few hours ago."

McCarthy looked around the room. "Maybe that's where our Mr. Wilson went."

"It's about 20 minutes from here. Should I have a car meet us there?"

"If they can get there before we can."

Julia pulled in front of Lizzie's house. Only one light was on inside. Julia took a deep breath to calm her racing heart. She checked her rearview mirror for the one-millionth time. She was positive no one followed her from her house, but that didn't mean he couldn't have come another way, especially if he already knew where Lizzie lived. On the drive over, Julia had made up her mind that she and Lizzie were going to have to go to the police together and tell them the whole story.

She knew Lizzie would resist, but Julia was convinced it was the only way they were going to stay alive with a madman on the loose.

He had already killed three people. What's to stop him from killing them, especially if they were the only living links to two of the other killings?

Julia waited and searched the street from the car. Everything was silent. It was about two hours from sunrise.

At this point, all she wanted to do was survive the rest of the night. They could deal with the rest of their lives later, in daylight.

Satisfied she was alone, Julia shut off the car and got out. She started walking toward the front door when she heard a shuffling sound behind her. She whirled around, wishing she had some kind of weapon. Her eyes scanned the bushes and trees lining the street and driveway leading up to Lizzie's garage.

Then she spotted the branch of a tree, being pushed along by a stiff breeze that was coming in from the Sound. The branch made a scratching sound on the pavement. Julia let out a deep sigh and continued on toward the front door.

She was about to push the buzzer when the door opened, giving her a start.

"Aggghhh!" cried Julia.

Lizzie was standing in the doorway holding a bottle of beer.

"What took you so long? I saw you pull up and I've been waiting here for about five minutes."

"Sorry. I wanted to make sure no one was following me," said Julia as she stepped inside.

"Come here, baby."

Julia walked toward Lizzie, who put her arms around her and gave her a warm hug. "It's gonna be all right," said Lizzie stroking Julia's hair.

Julia let herself be held for about a minute and then pulled away. She turned and looked at Lizzie. "He's a killer, Lizzie. I'm sorry I didn't warn you. I didn't know until it was too late. We have to get out of here. He knows where you live."

"Hold on. Let's start from the beginning," said Lizzie, taking Julia by the hand and leading her into the living room. "Now, why do you think the man I shot in the head and then buried under a lake full of water is still alive?"

32

CHIEF MANZINI'S calves were aching by the time he reached the top of the steep stairway leading to Eddie the Hand's office. The crime scene unit was there in full force, dusting, infrared scoping and collecting fibers. The Medical Examiner was behind the corpse, now sprawled across a chair behind the office desk. He saw Manzini and nodded for him to approach.

"He was shot at close range, but I don't think this was any professional hit. The weapon was a .22, flat head, similar to what we find in contract killings, but this was a face on shot, not behind the ear," explained the M.E. "It's not the kind of shot a pro would have taken. Too much room for error. The only reason he's dead is that the shot entered the skull through the left eye. If it had hit the cranial cavity, there's a good chance it would have been deflected."

"You get the slug?"

"We got it."

"Good work."

Lizzie stared at Julia, not able to believe what she was hearing. She took a swig of beer and put the bottle down.

"You went back to the reservoir? Why?"

Julia had trouble looking her friend in the eye. She forced herself to go on.

"To find my watch."

"Your watch?"

"It has my name and Paul's engraved on the back. I thought it fell off in the car when I took the man's pulse. So we went back to the lake to look for it. That's when we discovered he was missing. I couldn't find my watch, either."

"I've gotta have a real drink." Lizzie stood up and went to a cabinet and took out a bottle of Chivas Regal. She opened the bottle and poured herself a full glass.

Returning to the table, she slammed her open hand down as hard as she could.

"And you didn't tell me!" Lizzie shouted, the rage causing her to spray saliva when she screamed.

"I'm sorry," said Julia.

"Sorry. Sorry. I don't believe this. You've know all this time that this guy I thought I killed might still be alive and you decided to keep this piece of information to yourselves? Julia. For God's sake, why?"

"After we found the car empty, we went home. I wanted to tell you but Paul talked me into waiting. He was still pissed at you, and I'd have to say I was angry, too."

"You were angry that I might have killed somebody but then you found out that maybe I didn't, so I don't get it. Why didn't you say something?"

"Well, we weren't sure. We thought maybe he just fell out. The back door of the car was open. We didn't think he was still alive until that stuff started to happen. You know, what you blamed Paul for."

"And that's what makes you think he's still alive?

"Well, yes. Look at everything that's happened. Paul getting shot and killed. John drinking the bleach. It has to be him."

"But Paul did really call me with his stupid blackmail scheme. I recognized his voice."

"I know. He was sorry about that. But he called after we knew the body was missing."

"I see. He figured it was okay to put the heat on us. Try to squeeze some money out of us. What made him think we had any money?"

"I don't know."

"I told you our situation, how much debt we're in."

"I know. He thought maybe you found something in the car. I don't know. Look. He knew he made a mistake. He was even going to apologize. But that's not the point. I'm talking about all this other stuff. Your Jeep. Paul getting shot. John dying. I was at the police station and saw his picture, Lizzie."

"Whose picture?"

"The Stranger's. The police were already looking for him."

"I knew it," said Lizzie. "Mafia, right?"

"Mafia? He killed his wife."

"He what?"

"Police think he killed his wife and now we've got this psycho after us. Oh, my God!"

"What?"

"Where's Brian?"

"At my grandmother's. He's safe."

"Lizzie. I'm sorry. I know I should have told you sooner. I didn't know what to do. But I do now. We have to

199

go to the police. We need their protection. He's not going to stop until we're all dead. I just know it."

"And we thought the guy was a mobster."

"A mobster? Monster's more like it. Lizzie, did you hear what I said? About going to the police?"

"Boy, I really know how to pick 'em don't I?"

"Lizzie, come on. We have to get out of here."

Lizzie responded by letting out a deep laugh.

"What's so funny?"

"I was just thinking about you going back to the reservoir to look for your watch. That must have been a sight. You go in bareback? Remember when we used to go skinny dipping?"

"Lizzie. This isn't time to reminisce. Come on."

"I can just imagine you swimming around down there bare-ass naked, looking for your watch," Lizzie said, slurring her words.

"Lizzie, you're getting drunk. We can't be drunk right now."

"Why not? I can't think of a better reason to get drunk. John's dead. Paul's dead. It's just you and me, babe, just like the old days."

"With one major difference. There's a maniac out there killing people and we're on his short list of victims to come."

"So let me get this straight," slurred Lizzie. "You're down there with the car and, what there's no body? So you assume he's alive and out there killing people. What if the body just fell out of the car? Or some snapping turtles got him. You know that reservoir is full of snapping turtles. They could rip your arm right off. They probably ate the son of a bitch."

"Then how do you explain everything that's happened?"

"Right," answered Lizzie, saluting with her glass of scotch before taking another drink. "Not to mention your watch. Wonder what ver happened to your precious watch?"

"You mean this?"

The sound of Bruce Wilson's voice made Lizzie spill her drink. Julia leapt up from her chair. "Aggghhhh!"

Bruce held the gold watch out in front of him. In his other hand was a gun and it was aimed at Lizzie.

"Oh, my God!" shouted Julia as she backed up to the wall of the kitchen.

Lizzie's eyes widened as she rose from the table and backed up to the counter. Bruce walked toward Lizzie. For the first time since she had ever known her, Julia saw fear in Lizzie's eyes. Fear and something else, an expression that Julia was sure she was misinterpreting.

"I believe you have something of mine," Bruce said to Lizzie.

Julia saw Lizzie's expression shift once again to one of cold determination. This was an expression Julia knew well and had seen many times, whenever Lizzie had made up her mind to confront whatever unpleasant situation lay before her. This did not, however, explain the words Julia had just heard. "You have something of mine." What could she have of his?

"Lizzie," said Julia. "What's he talking about?"

"Got me, darlin'," said Lizzie ,as her hand felt along the counter top for a drawer.

"Please stop moving your hand," ordered Bruce. "I'll tell you what she has. An envelope with a considerable amount of money in it, and a ring. I'd like them back," said Bruce.

"Lizzie?" pleaded Julia. Was Paul right all this time? Had Lizzie and John held something back from them?

"I don't know what he's talking about."

Bruce cocked the gun and fired, blowing a hole out of one of the cabinets shattering some plates.

Julia closed her eyes. This was it. They were going to die. She felt as if she might faint when instead of another shot, she heard a calming voice.

"Take a moment to remember," he said, cocking the gun again.

"Lizzie. Please," begged Julia. "Give him what he wants. He's going to kill us."

"How do you know he isn't going to kill us anyway?"

"I just want my money and ring," said Bruce.

"I don't have...."

He waited a couple of seconds, then shot the sink. Dishwater began pouring out onto the floor of the kitchen. He aimed at the microwave and shot it through the glass front, spraying the corner with splinters of glass and metal.

"Okay! Stop shooting!" screamed Lizzie. "Okay!"

33

THE LIGHTS were off in Julia Stanton's house when Officer Larson and Detective McCarthy pulled into her driveway. The moon had gone down over the trees and the early morning sky was pitch black. Detective McCarthy had his service revolver drawn as he climbed out of the passenger side before the car had come to a complete stop. A light fog had crawled in through the houses and yards.

As McCarthy approached the front of the house, he saw the crime scene tape crossing the front door and streaming out along the hedges leading away from the door in both directions.

Larson turned off the car and joined McCarthy. He turned on his flashlight.

"Look at this," said McCarthy, nodding toward the garage. The door was still open and garbage was strewn across the garage floor. Plastic bags had been ripped open by an animal with sharp claws. Larson tried the door leading from the garage to the house but it was locked.

"Let's try around back," suggested McCarthy.

They set off in opposite directions. Officer Larson turned off his light and closed his eyes to adjust to the darkness. He listened carefully to pick up any unusual sounds. It was very quiet. Even the insects that hissed and chirped to each other during the rest of the night were asleep at this hour.

In the rear of the house, Larson found McCarthy looking through a large floor to ceiling sliding door. He pushed it slightly, and it opened. Larson stepped through first, turning on his flashlight, and holding his revolver in line with the light beam as he searched the room.

McCarthy followed him and quickly examined the neatly kept family room. There was a small, 20-inch television and VCR combo, next to a CD player and small sound system.

Larson headed up the stairs to the main level of the split-level home.

"Hello," cried out Larson. "Anybody home? Mrs. Stanton? It's Officer Larson."

McCarthy found a light switch and turned on the lights. On a mantel over the fireplace, there were a series of photographs. The pictures were of the same four people, taken at different years in the recent past, four friends smiling for the camera. McCarthy felt a chill as he realized that two of the people in the pictures were no longer alive. One had been shot, and the other dead from an apparent accidental poisoning. A thought exploded in his detective's mind. Are the deaths related? Did I get here too late?

McCarthy looked around the room for answers and when he didn't find any, he followed Larson upstairs.

Larson was in the living room, behind the crime scene tape.

"Doesn't look like she's here," he said. "I checked all the bedrooms, bathrooms, closets."

McCarthy nodded at the crime scene tape. "This where he was shot?"

"Actually, he was shot in the foyer, just inside the front door. We sealed off the living room to search for the slug, but we haven't found it yet. Might be in one of the chairs or the sofa. The crime scene unit was called away to another shooting and had to stop the search. They'll be back later today."

"What do you think? Maybe she decided to stay with relatives."

"When I brought her back here I had the impression she intended to stay."

"Looks like she changed her mind."

"Could you blame her? Somebody comes to your house. Kills your husband. I think I'd wanta sleep somewhere else."

"But where? And what's her connection to Bruce Wilson?" asked McCarthy.

"Maybe they were having an affair. Maybe he killed her husband."

"That would explain her reaction to seeing his photo at the police station."

"Didn't I hear that Wilson killed his wife?"

"It looks that way. We're still waiting for the coroner to issue an official cause of death ruling."

"Well, if he killed once," said Larson, "there sure as hell ain't much to stop him from killing again."

"That's why I'm here, my boy," said McCarthy.

"I hate to say this, sir, but appears you got here a little late."

"You're not saying anything that I haven't already thought, son. Right now I just want to do whatever possible to stop him from killing anyone else."

"Like Mrs. Stanton."

34

WITH THE SMELL of cordite still wafting through the small house, Lizzie led the way to her bedroom. Julia was right behind her and Bruce was behind both of them holding the gun, its barrel still smoking from his recent shooting expedition in the kitchen.

Julia tried real hard not to look terrified, but the harder she tried, the more scared she felt. She thought she would wet her pants any second. The tension was becoming unbearable. She was certain that she and Lizzie were dead women walking. That this man had already murdered his wife, her husband, Lizzie's husband and God knew who else. Her mind raced to explore possible means of escape, but nothing came clear. Had this been a nightmare, she would have forced herself awake. But this nightmare was real and no solution seemed possible. Then she remembered a move she'd seen once. It was *The Deer Hunter* starring Robert DeNiro. He was in a Vietnamese prisoner of war camp being forced to play Russian Roulette with his fellow prisoners. He was as trapped as Julia felt now. But he managed to escape by taking a bad situation and making it worse. Instead of putting only one bullet in a chamber, he asked for more bullets, and left only one chamber empty. He then used the extra bullets to shoot his captors instead of himself. He made things worse in order to make them better. What did she have to lose?

"You're not going to get away with this," Julia spat out. "The police know you're here. They've got your picture."

"How do you know what the police have?" asked Bruce.

"I saw it. At the police station. It was on a computer. They've got you. They're probably on their way here right now. "

"Really. Well, right now, I've got you," replied Bruce. "And if you want to survive this night, you'll do what I say."

"Ya know, if you hadn't tried to kidnap my friend none of this would have happened," said Julia.

Julia saw a perplexed expression wash over Bruce's face.

"Kidnap? Is that what she told you?" he said, shaking his head.

Lizzie walked across the room to her closet.

"You are the one who locked me in your car and took off," said Lizzie from across the room. "What would you call it?"

Bruce and Julia were just inside the door of the small bedroom. Lizzie stood in front of a closet. Bruce looked at

Julia, who was trying to position herself to grab Bruce's gun should she ever get the chance.

"I'd call it survival. After all, you and your husband had just tried to rob me," said Bruce.

The words sent a chill down Julia's spine and she looked over at Lizzie, who rolled her eyes and shook her head.

"Is that true?" asked Julia.

"How could you even ask me such a question?" said Lizzie as she opened the closet door and knelt down. "He's a wife killer. And now he's going to kill us."

"All I want is my money and ring," said Bruce. "I'm not going to kill anyone."

Julia turned toward Bruce.

"The police said you killed your wife."

"It was an accident," said Bruce, the color draining from his face. "I didn't mean to kill her. I didn't even hit her that hard. She fell and hit her head on the counter. I feel sick about it. I'd do anything to turn back the clock."

"So put your gun away and turn yourself in," said Julia.

"I'm not ready to do that yet," said Bruce.

"No. He's going to kill us first," said Lizzie.

"Not if you do as I say," said Bruce, who had the saddest expression Julia had ever seen.

"Oh right. Yeah, sure. You're gonna let us live, especially after we pushed you in the lake. We tried to kill you. You could have drowned," said Julia.

"You thought I was already dead," said Bruce, now looking at Julia. "I heard you talking. I also know that you didn't want to be a part of it. You tried to help me. I heard it all. I pretended to be dead. I even meditated to slow my pulse. An old trick from my hippie days. Anyway, right now, all I want is my money and my ring and I'm gone. I'll probably have to tie you two up or something, but I have no intention of killing either of you- even if there would be a certain amount of justice for your friend to be executed. But you know, I don't even blame her for all she's done. I blame myself. I'm the one who deserves to die."

"I'm just curious," said Lizzie, still bent over and rummaging in the closet. "That ring."

"What about it?"

"How much is it worth?"

"It was appraised at forty-five-hundred dollars."

"Lizzie?" said Julia. "Did you really take his ring?"

"Your girlfriend took more than that, didn't you?" said Bruce. "I had about thirty-thousand dollars cash in the glove compartment."

"Paul was right," said Julia.

"We thought he was dead, remember?" said Lizzie, her back still toward them. "Okay, so I found some money in his glove compartment. I figured he wasn't going to need it anymore. I was gonna use it to pay off Eddie the Hand. We were going to be out of debt, Julia. Do you know how that feels? The freedom. It's like we've been living in slavery for the past five years, with the chains getting heavier each year that we owed more money to that scumbag. What was it you said? That you deserve to die."

With that, Lizzie stood up and turned around, holding her gun and pointing it at Bruce.

"I got a better idea," said Bruce. "Why don't we just kill each other?"

"Stop!" screamed Julia.

"You should've stayed dead," said Lizzie.

"You're probably right there."

Julia couldn't believe what she was hearing. She looked back and forth between Bruce and Lizzie. "You're both crazy."

"You don't really care if I shoot you, do you?" said Lizzie.

"Not really. How about you?"

"I don't want to die. At least not yet."

"Then put your gun down."

"Why should I do that?"

"So you can live," said Bruce.

"How about if I do this?" said Lizzie, as she turned and aimed her gun at Julia.

"Lizzie!" gasped Julia.

"Now, if you don't put your gun down, I'm gonna shoot her, and she's my best friend."

Bruce looked at Julia and saw the terror in her eyes.

"You'd really do that?" he said. "I don't believe you."

"Julia knows me better than anyone," said Lizzie. "What do you say, darlin? Would I shoot you?"

Julia looked from Bruce to Lizzie and back to Bruce.

"Oh God, Lizzie."

"Okay," said Bruce. "Go ahead. Shoot her. And then I'll just shoot you and walk out of here."

"The hell you will. Now put the goddamn gun down," screamed Lizzie, the veins on her neck straining from the fury. Her face took on a demonic expression as her eyes glared red with rage.

"I can't. Besides, if I do that you'll just shoot me."

"It's either you or her. Make up your mind. Cause somebody's sure as shit's gonna die tonight."

Bruce turned to look at Julia and saw the tears running down her face. This woman with the gun was crazy. She was willing to kill her best friend and her friend knew it. His heart went out to this poor woman, who had shown nothing but compassion to him until tonight. He couldn't let it go on any longer. The killing had to stop here. If anyone else was going to die, it was going to be him. He lowered his head and then lowered his gun in defeat.

As soon as Bruce pointed his gun toward the floor, Lizzie shifted her aim.

Julia couldn't believe her friend was going to shoot. "No!" screamed Julia.

The explosion filled the room as Lizzie fired.

The bullet slammed into Bruce's stomach, causing him to double over, but not fall down. Bruce dropped his gun and looked down at the small hole in his shirt.

Slowly, blood began to seep from the hole and darken the area around his shirt. He looked up at Lizzie and then at Julia, who just stared back at him, confusion and pain pulling at her face.

Bruce opened his mouth to speak but instead collapsed to the floor.

Julia let out a giant sigh and slumped against the bedroom wall. Lizzie ran to her and held her by the shoulders.

"Are you all right? I'm sorry."

Julia looked at her friend's face, into her eyes. A coldness wrapped itself around Julia's heart.

"Julia, baby, it was the only way out of this. Please believe me."

"You were going to shoot me."

"I wouldn't. I couldn't. Come on, I need your help. We have to get him out to your car."

"What?"

"We can't just let him lay there. My rental's too small. We'll take your car."

"Why not just call the police? They're looking for him anyway," said Julia.

"This will be better."

"I don't understand."

"You wanta go to jail?"

"Jail? Why would we go to jail?"

"Because we're alive and he's dead."

"That's the kind of stupid thinking that started this whole mess. Well, not this time, Lizzie. I'm calling the police."

Julia took a cellular phone out of her jacket pocket, along with Detective Burger's card. Lizzie moved in close and snapped the phone out of Julia's hand. She hurled it against the wall. The plastic phone smashed into a dozen pieces. Lizzie then pressed the muzzle of her gun against Julia's cheek.

"I'm starting to lose my patience with you. We're going to take a little ride. Now you can either be part of the problem or part of the solution. It's your choice."

Julia stared down at the gun. She could feel the muzzle's heat burning her skin.

"It's just you and me, Julia," said Lizzie. "John's gone. So's Paul. We need each other. More than ever. Don't turn on me now."

35

DETECTIVE MCCARTHY and Officer Larson returned to the lower level of Julia's house and were turning off the lights, when McCarthy walked over to the fireplace mantel. He picked up one of the photographs and walked over to Larson.

"What is it?"

"If you were going to stay with someone other than family, who would you seek out?"

"A friend?"

"This couple maybe," said McCarthy, showing the photo to Larson.

"Lizzie and John Daly. Holy shit!"

"What?"

"That's the fellow we brought in last night. Or was it earlier this morning. I forget."

"What do mean, brought in?"

"His body. According to his wife, he apparently accidentally drank some bleach."

"I bet that's where she is," said McCarthy.

"Let's go. They live over on Orchard Street. It's about ten minutes from here."

As they climbed into the car, McCarthy had a nagging thought.

"Don't you think it's a little suspicious?"

"What's that?" said Larson, as he put the cruiser in gear and backed out of the driveway.

"That two spouses of two couples die within hours of each other."

"Yeah, but one was shot and the other one accidentally drank some bleach. What's the connection to that?"

"How do we know he accidentally drank anything?"

"We found the two glasses. Only his prints were on them. One contained vodka, the other bleach."

"Who puts bleach in a drinking glass?"

"He was doing laundry."

"So why not just pour it in the washer. Why put it into a glass first?"

"To measure it?"

"It was a drinking glass. Not a measuring cup."

"Okay, let's say they're connected," said Larson. "How? Why? What's the motive?"

"We have to talk to the wives," said McCarthy. "I think it all ties to Wilson. He had a similar photo in his hotel room."

Larson stopped the car at a red light. McCarthy had the photograph in his lap. He held it up and looked at the faces.

"Who are these people?" McCarthy asked.

"Just everyday people, sir," said Larson.

"Everyday people. What's that supposed to mean?"

"Well, Julia Stanton, she's an oral hygienist. Her husband worked at a gas station."

"And the other two?"

"John Daly was a carpenter and his wife's a beautician and part-time waitress."

"Doesn't get more everyday than that, does it?"

"What about Wilson?" asked Larson.

"That's the kicker," said McCarthy. "He's just a computer salesman. So here's the question, Officer Larson. How come five everyday people are involved in three homicides?"

"Three?"

"I threw Wilson's wife in there."

"Well, we don't know if Daly was homicide."

"Okay. Three suspicious deaths, then. Whatever it is, it just doesn't happen everyday, is all I'm saying."

The light changed, and Larson started to make a left turn. As he did, another car, approaching from the opposite direction, made a legal right turn on the red light. As the two cars passed, Larson looked in the rear view at the other vehicle and slammed on the brakes.

"What is it?" asked McCarthy.

"I believe the Buick that just turned back there is Julia Stanton's car."

36

IT WAS HAPPENING all over again. Julia was driving and Lizzie was sitting next to her with her gun in her hand. The only difference this time was that Paul and John were no longer with them. Julia wondered what jumbled-up circuit in Lizzie's brain caused her to think like this? It was a question Julia had asked nearly all their lives, or at least as long as she knew Lizzie. Despite the insanity, Julia still had feelings of warmth for her friend. Even now, after she was sure Lizzie would have shot her. Who was crazier, Lizzie or me? Julia asked herself. As she watched the now-familiar trees pass by, Julia's sense of déjà vu went into overdrive. How, she wondered, would this trip to Mystery Lake play out? In all their years together, Julia always felt she could ultimately control her friend's turbulent nature. Now, as she drove along in silence, she began to wonder if Lizzie had crossed into some unreachable universe, where only the psychotic survive, where nothing is real beyond the internal struggle in a nightmare that never ends.

Julia glanced into the back seat where Bruce Wilson was either dead or bleeding to death. Lizzie knocked on the glass of her door window.

"Okay, turn here."

Julia turned off the main highway and started down the side road that ran parallel to the reservoir.

A realization sent a shiver down Julia's spine. She turned toward Lizzie.

"You're going to kill me, too, aren't you."

Lizzie's eyes filled with water. "Just shut up and drive."

Back on the main highway, the police cruiser carrying Detective McCarthy and Officer Larson sped past the turnoff to the reservoir.

Detective McCarthy stared at the empty highway ahead leading out of town. Something was wrong.

"Where'd they go?" asked McCarthy.

"They were just ahead of us, not more than a mile," said Larson. "I saw their lights."

"So where are they now?"

Larson put his foot on the brakes and the car skidded to a stop.

"They must have turned off somewhere along here," said the patrolman.

Slowly, he began to back up. "Roll down your window. Listen for an engine."

As the car backed up, McCarthy rolled down his window and put his head out into the early morning air. He could smell the salt coming in on the fog from Long Island Sound.

McCarthy heard it first. The faint sound of an engine.

"Over there," said McCarthy. They looked down a side road and saw a pair of taillights. Larson gunned the engine and the car sped off down a side road.

The cruiser reached 70 miles an hour as it bumped and churned over the gravel, one-lane road. They were coming up on the taillights fast, when the lights got brighter as the driver applied brakes and began to turn into a driveway. The cruiser came to a skidding, sliding stop, spraying gravel and sand onto the side of the road.

They stared at the red pickup truck and the scared woman who was getting out carrying a lunch box.

"Sorry ma'am," shouted Larson, as he hit the accelerator and drove them back to the main road to continue their search for another possible route.

It was the same spot where they had pushed the white car into the reservoir. Julia stopped her car on the same rise and shifted into park. She also put the parking brake on, just in case.

Julia turned toward Lizzie.

"It's not too late. We could still go to the police."

"But it is too late. Don't you understand? Don't you know what you've done?"

"What I've done?"

"It's such a pity," said Lizzie sadly. "All you had to do was tell me you went back."

"I said I was sorry."

"None of this had to happen. All you had to do was tell me the car was empty."

"How would that have made a difference, Lizzie? I don't follow you."

"You don't realize what you did? Your silence killed them."

"Killed who?"

"Paul, John, him. Even Eddie."

"Eddie?"

"And you wonder why we can't go to the police. Julia, we killed four people."

"Lizzie, you're not making sense."

"You're right. We didn't kill them. You killed them, Julia."

"I don't ... Oh, my God."

"Do you see it now?" said Lizzie. "If you had only told me the truth, I wouldn't have had to do it. But I couldn't take any chances, especially after Paul called me and threatened to go to the police if I didn't share the money."

"It was you."

"And then John. You know how John could never keep his mouth shut about anything. Eventually he would have told one of his asshole drinking buddies about the man we dumped in the reservoir. I was eliminating possible witnesses to a murder. Only there never was a murder. At least not then. Unfortunately, now we have several, which will be even harder to cover up, but then the only two people left who know what happened are right here."

"Lizzie, please."

"If only I'd known he wasn't even dead. They'd all be alive and we wouldn't be here. And I wouldn't have to do what I have to do. So I do hold you responsible, Julia. You could have prevented three deaths. Well, at least two. Eddie the Hand. Who knows? I might have had to do him, anyway. But John and Paul. They'd be alive, for sure."

Julia felt herself get dizzy. She had to fight it. She couldn't faint. Suddenly, she felt an enormous weight. She wanted to die. What Lizzie had said rang true. She was responsible. Please forgive me, Paul. Oh God. How can I make this right? Suddenly, Julia could no longer control her tears and she began to weep.

"Oh Julia, get a hold of yourself. Come on. Out of the car."

Detective McCarthy's neck was starting to strain from looking out the window at the passing countryside. Officer Larson stopped the car when they came to a side road.

"Where's that go?"

"That's the maintenance road for the old lake."

"Lake?"

"Yeah. Mystery Lake. We use it for a reservoir now. Nobody lives down there, though. Years ago there used to be weekend houses."

With Lizzie pointing her gun at her back, Julia dragged Bruce from the car to the bank of the reservoir. She had to stop and catch her breath.

"He's too heavy," said Julia as she let him down on the gravel hill.

"Take off your clothes," said Lizzie.

"What?"

"You heard me. Strip."

Lizzie walked over to Julia holding the gun on her. She put the barrel next to Julia's head and cocked the trigger.

"Do it."

"Lizzie, don't do this."

"Come on."

Julia began to tremble as she unbuttoned her blouse and slipped it off. Then she unsnapped her wet blue jeans and pulled them down, along with her underwear. Stepping out of her sneakers, she pulled the jeans and panties the rest of the way off. Lizzie put the barrel of the gun under Julia's bra strap and tugged. Julia unsnapped her bra and let it fall to the ground.

Julia tried to cover her breasts and pubic area.

"Julia. Stop acting like I ain't ever seen you naked before. We take showers together at the gym."

"You never had a gun pointed at me before."

"Is that what's making you go shy on me? This little old gun. Powerful little sucker, ain't it? Almost like I got a dick. A big old powerful dick. A life or death dick. I could make you my love slave. How does that sound? But then how long would that last? Sooner or later, I'd have to kill you. Better do it now before I fall even deeper in love with you. I bet you didn't even know how I felt about you, did you, Julia? I do. I used to fantasize about you when I was making love with John or whenever I masturbated. You were the one I was with. You made me come. You could make me come right now, but goddamnit. I have to kill you. Do you know how much that hurts? What was that?"

Julia hadn't even heard it. She was in too much shock to hear anything other than Lizzie's voice.

"There." Lizzie turned toward the faint sound of a car engine.

As soon as Lizzie turned, moving her aim away from Julia's head, Julia pushed Lizzie as hard as she could, knocking her down. Julia then ran and dove into the lake just as Lizzie got her footing and began shooting down into the water.

Julia swam straight down into the black water. Over her shoulder, a bullet ripped through the water just past her neck. She could feel the pressure from the water that the bullet made as it passed within an inch of her.

Her powerful arms and legs pulled her deeper into the lake, until she was now on the floor, about twenty feet beneath the surface and looking up.

It was then that she saw a hypnotic sight. A bullet was speeding through the water like a torpedo and it was moving right at her face. The bullet was about a yard in front of her when she moved to the side and it went past where her head used to be.

Julia felt as if her lungs were going to burst as she followed the floor of the lake deeper. As she backed farther away from shore, she could see Lizzie's silhouette on shore and the flares of orange as the gun barrel exploded with each shot. Three more bullets began churning through the water at Julia. She was never going to be able to dodge all three, so she scrambled as fast and as deep she could. Three were coming right at her as Julia let herself sink lower and lower. She closed her eyes, waiting for the impact. Bracing for the slugs to tear into her flesh. She opened her eyes just in time to see one of the bullets hit her stomach just above the belly button. She flinched, but the bullet didn't penetrate the skin. Instead, it just stung her and then rolled off into the darkness of the water. She looked up as another bullet came right at her face. It was going to hit her left eye. But it dropped about an inch before it hit and fell down her check like an iron tear. The third bullet landed on her shoulder and rolled off.

She looked up at the shore and it was empty. Feeling herself about to pass out from lack of oxygen and the need to open her lungs, she swam to the surface.

Julia's head broke the surface and she gasped for breath. She looked around, expecting Lizzie to finish her off, but no one was there. A tremor of relief shook her body. Julia crawled onto the bank and saw Bruce, lying still. There was something in Bruce's hand. It was Lizzie's gun. Julia pried the gun from Bruce's fingers and was trying to decide what to do with it when she heard a car engine and the crunch of tires on gravel.

A horrible thought flashed through Julia's mind. Lizzie's come back. Julia checked the gun. It was empty. Shit. She heard footsteps behind her and she whirled around holding the empty gun out.

"Stop!" she screamed.

Detective McCarthy put his hands up but Officer Larson pulled his weapon and dropped to a one-knee firing position.

"Drop the weapon, Mrs. Stanton."

Julia dropped the gun immediately. "Thank God," she said, and then realized she was naked. She quickly put her arms over her breasts and used Bruce as a shield for the lower part of her body.

Detective McCarthy put his hands down and approached Julia cautiously.

"Please turn around, ma'am." She did, and he pulled her hands behind her and put a pair of plastic cuffs around her wrist.

"She's getting away," shouted Julia.

"Just be still, ma'am," said McCarthy.

Officer Larson checked Bruce, feeling his neck. "He's still alive. But just barely."

"Okay, you stay with him. I'll call for the paramedics and a squad car to take her in."

From the back seat of a police cruiser, Julia, wearing a scratchy wool blanket and handcuffs, watched as a paramedic fed Bruce oxygen and blood, while another one wrapped a bandage around his stomach. They then strapped him to a gurney and carried him to an ambulance.

Lizzie was out there somewhere, hiding in the woods. Julia's Buick was being impounded. Its front end was hoisted off the ground by a tow truck. Officer Larson got behind the wheel of the cruiser and Detective McCarthy got into the passenger side.

On the horizon, dawn was breaking as the sun began to appear behind the trees on the far side of the reservoir. Julia looked up and saw Officer Larson looking back at her through the rearview mirror.

"You've got to believe me," pleaded Julia. "Lizzie Daly shot that man. And she tried to shoot me."

Larson put the car in gear and pulled away from the reservoir.

"I'm sorry Mrs. Stanton," said Larson. "But we have to take you in. Put everything you have to say in a statement and we'll try to get someone to verify it. But until then, we gonna have to hold you in custody. I'm sorry ma'am."

Julia lowered her head. The sound of an engine got her attention and she looked up just as the ambulance sped off into the night. She said a silent prayer that Bruce Wilson would survive.

She then leaned her head back and took in a deep breath. At least she was still alive.

First, a patrol car with Julia in the back sped by, followed by an ambulance, a tow truck, and then another police cruiser. From her spot in the bushes, Lizzie could see everything. A mosquito landed on her arm and she waited for it to draw some blood before she mashed it on her skin.

The sun had broken through the trees and Lizzie looked up at the red sky. She let out a sigh and began walking through the forest.

"See, Julia," she said aloud. "I told you they'd put you in jail."

It was Officer Larson who brought her the news. She could hear his footsteps in the hallway outside her cell before she knew who it was. Julia had spent two days in the cell, wondering what was going on in the rest of the world. The two days seemed like an eternity. No formal charges had been filed yet against Julia. Still, they kept her in jail as long as they could, which was about to expire if they didn't arraign her. Julia was at the cell's only window when she turned and saw the guard with Officer Larson. The guard unlocked her cell.

"Mrs. Stanton," said Officer Larson. He had a sheepish expression on his face as if he was embarrassed about doing his job.

Julia looked like she had the life drained out of her.

225

"How is he? Is he dead? Is that why you're here? To tell me he's dead?"

Officer Larson stepped into the small cell. "No, ma'am. In fact, Mr. Wilson is fine. He's regained consciousness."

"Oh, that's great," said Julia. She slumped against the wall of her cell.

"Mrs. Stanton, I just want to say, we owe you an apology," said Officer Larson. "Mr. Wilson corroborated your story. We're letting you go. No charges will be filed."

Julia looked at Officer Larson and then the guard. Without being able to stop herself, she sat down on the narrow bed and cried. Officer Larson let her sob for a couple of minutes before clearing his throat.

"Ah, Mrs. Stanton?"

"Yes," said Julia wiping her eyes and looking up.

"There's something else you should know, about Mr. Wilson."

"What?"

"It turns out he didn't kill his wife after all."

"You're kidding. What happened?"

"She had some kind of brain aneurysm. I'll let Mr. Wilson fill you in on the details. He's been asking for you ever since he regained consciousness."

37

BRUCE WILSON was sitting up in his hospital bed reading the local paper when Julia knocked on the door of his private room. His head and abdomen were heavily bandaged.

Julia hesitated in the doorway as Bruce slowly lowered his paper.

"Hi," said. 'Come in."

Julia entered the tiny room, which was barely large enough for the single hospital bed. She carried a shopping bag in one hand and a bouquet of flowers—carnations, irises, roses, and ferns—in a glass vase that still bore the sticker of the first floor hospital gift shop in the other. Julia removed the sticker and put the vase of flowers on the windowsill.

"They're beautiful," said Bruce.

"Thanks," said Julia. "I also got you these." She reached into the shopping bag and pulled out a box of Russell Stover candies, a stack of magazines, *People, Time,* and *Newsweek.* She placed them on a Formica table next to his bed.

"This is a nice surprise," said Bruce, as a big smile spread across his exhausted face.

Julia felt like running from the room as fast as she could, but she forced herself to stay. She was here to make amends, and by God, that's what she was going to do. She saw the fatigue in his face and wondered if she should just let him rest.

"Maybe I should go. You look real tired."

"No," pleaded Bruce. "Don't go. Sit down."

"Are you sure? I could come back. You should get some rest."

"That's all I've been doing, but it doesn't help," said Bruce. "I'd rather talk. I need to talk."

Julia moved around the end of the bed and sat in the only chair in the room, which was wedged between the bed and the interior wall.

"I just wanted to thank you. If it weren't for you, I'd still be in jail. I also want to apologize for all the trouble we caused you," said Julia, her head bowed so she didn't have to look at his face.

"Trouble? You saved my life," said Bruce.

Julia looked up and shook her head. "I wish that were true Mr. Wilson."

"Please, call me Bruce. It *is* true."

"It may have seemed that way, but I was really just trying to save myself," said Julia, feeling a mixture of shame and relief.

"Well, in the process you saved me, too, and I will be eternally grateful."

"Grateful? All I want is your forgiveness."

"Forgiveness for what?"

"For what we did to you. We tried to kill you by pushing your car into the lake."

"But you thought I was already dead. Besides, you didn't help them push the car."

"I didn't stop them either."

"You couldn't."

"I didn't even try. "

"Here's what I remember," said Bruce. "I remember feeling your warm hand on my wrist when you tried to find my pulse. I remember playing dead and trying hard not to move. I did peek once or twice. I saw that she had a gun out and was pointing it at you."

"You saw all that?"

"What I didn't see, I heard."

Julia almost smiled as she compared Bruce's version of that fateful first night at the reservoir to her own recollection. She wanted to accept his assessment. It would be so comforting since they felt so close to her own. Her memory had been altered by the torturous incidents that had followed. But if she could accept Bruce's interpretation, she just might be able to absolve herself of the guilt she felt about Paul's murder. Oh how she wanted to do that more than anything. She missed her husband deeply. In fact, she felt more for him now than she ever did when he was alive. His death left a void so deep it had no bottom. And Julia felt totally alone. As if he could feel her feelings Bruce reached out and put his hand on hers.

"I wanted to die," he continued. "But you didn't know that. I thought I'd killed my wife and wanted to die, to be with her. So I was going to let you people push my car into the lake. I was going to let myself drown. But something happened down there in that black water. I heard my daughter's voice. And then I saw her all alone, and suddenly I knew that I couldn't let myself drown. So as soon as the car went under, I opened a door and crawled out. I swam as far away as possible before coming up for air. You were all standing on the bank looking at where the car went down so you didn't see me. Everybody always said I was hardheaded. Guess I proved them right. The bullet apparently just grazed my skull, but severed a vessel. That's where all the bleeding came from. The doctors said my temporary amnesia was caused by lack of blood to the brain. It sure gave one hell of a headache, I can tell you that."

"I'm sorry about your wife," said Julia.

"Thank you."

"The police told me what happened. That you hit her, but that the blow wasn't what caused her death. She had some kind of brain disease."

"I thought she was having an affair," said Bruce, tears filling his eyes. "I could sense she was keeping something from me. She'd been sneaking out and didn't know I knew she was doing it. Only it turns out she'd been sneaking out to see a neurologist. Then she said she wanted a divorce. I was sure she'd found somebody else. She never told me about the headaches. She was going to leave me so I wouldn't have to see her die."

Julia felt her eyes fill with tears and for the next few minutes they cried together in silence. Julia turned her hand over and he squeezed his palm into hers.

"What's your daughter's name?" asked Julia, pushing back her tears.

"Lisa," said Bruce, his face regaining some color. "Her aunt's bringing her to the hospital today. They should get here soon. I'd like you to meet them."

A rush of panic gripped Julia and she stood up from the chair.

"I don't think so. I couldn't. Not yet."

"Why not?"

"I don't know," said Julia, moving toward the door. "I still feel as if I need to be punished. I know what you said, but it's not that easy. I still feel responsible and that's something I'm going to have to deal with on my own. Anyway, I just stopped by to say thanks and that I'm sorry for any trouble I may have caused you."

"Please," said Bruce. "Don't leave."

"I have to," said Julia. "There's something I have to take care of."

"Will I see you again?"

"I don't know. I have to go."

Julia ran from the room.

38

JULIA RAN DOWN the hospital corridor, found a crowd waiting for the elevators, and took the stairs down four flights to the main lobby. She rushed out into the bright noon-day sun. What was she running from? What happened up there that should cause so much anxiety? Julia wasn't sure. All she knew was that her adrenal system was on overload, pumping a virtual cocktail of hormones into her system, causing her to hyperventilate.

She had to sit down, to breathe deeply, and to soothe the terror rushing through her body. The title of a book she had seen once in the library flashed in her mind's screen: *Emotional Intelligence.* Was this a joke? An oxymoron. I'm the moron, thought Julia. Why was it that whenever her emotions took over, intelligence was the first casualty? She was beyond rational thinking. Too many emotions were colliding all at once, and all she wanted to do was crawl into bed, any bed, and make it all go away. She thought she might vomit any second now, and that would be good. But when she tried to bring something up, her stomach was empty and nothing came up.

She looked at her hand and could still feel his touch. She tried to rub it away, but it wouldn't leave. It was as if he branded her somehow.

The poor man, she thought. All this time, thinking he'd killed his wife, when it was something so far from his control, or capacity. But you, Julia. You are not so innocent, are you? It was your silence that caused your husband to lose his life. His death was something that could have been prevented. By you!

The guilt was unrelenting as it tore though her heart. She now knew how Bruce felt that night in the car, for she too wanted to die. To pay for her sins. But she would not go alone. There was someone else who had to share in the punishment. And Julia vowed to herself that she would devote every waking moment to see that justice was served.

"I ... I'd like to see you again." Bruce's voice echoed in her ears.

Maybe, thought Julia, in another life. For now, there was much work to do. She had to prepare for Lizzie's return. And Julia knew her friend would be back. She'd left her son with her grandmother. She would come back for him. And Julia would be ready.

The next three days passed quickly for Julia. There was a simple funeral and burial for Paul, attended by Julia and some of Paul's co-workers at the service station. Paul had never written a will, so Julia assumed possession of their joint property. On the day following the burial, with less than $700 remaining in their checking account, Julia returned to work. She had the office schedule as many cleanings as she could handle to help pay off the funeral costs. When she wasn't working, she sat alone in her house staring at the television without actually comprehending what was on. It was white noise in an otherwise black world. She spent one whole day cleaning the house, washing every surface with disinfectant.

Over the following week, a couple of friends called to express their condolences, and then she received a letter from Bruce, who had left the hospital and had returned to Huntington. She didn't open the letter. Everyday, she called Lizzie's phone and listened to her answering machine tell her to leave a message. Occasionally, she checked with the police to see if anyone had spotted her friend, or if she had been taken into custody. Nothing. Julia had learned that police had put Lizzie's house under 24-hour surveillance.

The only place Julia felt whole was in the dental office, where she could put her skills to use in the service of others. She became totally absorbed in the process, turning the scraping and cleaning into a ritual of near religious proportions. Between cleanings, she practiced in secret something forbidden in the eyes of the Connecticut Department of Health Services.

Locked behind a door, in a rear storage room, Julia removed the plastic packaging around the sterile hypodermic needle, pulled off the long narrow cap covering the metal part of the needle, held up a vial of novocaine, and inserted the needle into the vial. After filling it with the local anesthetic, she plunged it into an orange. She repeated this two or three more times before returning to the dental office where her next cleaning patient was waiting.

After eating dinner alone at the Lakeside Diner, Julia returned home as late as she could. The waitress who had replaced Lizzie had just moved to Lakeside and was new to the area. She didn't know Julia and Julia was thankful for that. She was tired of retelling the story to acquaintances of the two couples who seemed to be everywhere. No one at the diner who knew Lizzie had seen her since her disappearance.

Back in her house, Julia turned on the TV for company and was surfing through channels when the phone rang.

She looked at it, wondering whether to answer. What if it was Bruce? She still wasn't ready to talk to him. What if it was Lizzie? Would she have the nerve to call her?

Julia answered her question by picking up the receiver.

"Hello."

"Mrs. Stanton, it's Officer Larson."

"Yes."

"You wanted us to alert you when we discontinued surveillance on the Daly residence."

"Has it been two weeks already?"

"Yes, ma'am. I tried to get the chief to extend it another week, but we're short-staffed as it is. We will be doing drive-byes now and then, just in case."

"Thanks for calling."

"My pleasure, ma'am. How are you doing, by the way?"

"I'm okay," Julia lied.

"Well, we're here if you need us."

"Thanks. Good night."

Julia hung up the phone. This was what she was waiting for. She knew Lizzie would also wait until the police surveillance stopped.

39

THE FOLLOWING MORNING, Julia called the dental office and told the receptionist to reschedule her appointments for the day. She wasn't feeling well and was taking a sick day. She then dressed in a light summer dress and grabbed her tote bag.

The drive from her house to Lizzie's grandmother's took about fifteen minutes. It felt like 15 days. On the trip over, she replayed potential scenarios, as well as whether she should alert the Lakeside police department of her suspicions: that Lizzie's first stop back in Lakeside would be her grandmother's to pick up her son Brian.

Julia stopped on the street without pulling into the driveway. There was a miniature lawn in front of the tiny house. In fact, one could probably call it more like a plot of grass rather than a lawn. A tricycle was on its side on the grass. To the side of the house, was a red plastic Little Tykes sliding board.

Julia knew the woman as Grandma Davis. She had been to the one-bedroom ranch house when she and Lizzie were kids and Grandma Davis was baby-sitting for Lizzie's mother. She remembered how petite the house was even then. Now, it looked even smaller.

Julia approached the front door and was about to knock when the door opened.

"What do you want?" snarled Grandma Davis, filling her doorway like a gargoyle.

"It's Julia Stanton, Mrs. Davis. You probably remember me as Julia…"

"I know who you are. What do you want?"

"Just stopped by to say hello."

"That's a crock and we both know it."

"How's Brian doing?"

"What's it to you?"

"I'm concerned, that's all."

"He's fine. Now leave us alone." Grandma Davis started to turn away and shut the door, but Julia stopped it with her foot.

"Please. I just want to talk to you."

"I got nothin to say to you."

"Mrs. Davis. I was Lizzie's best friend."

"I told you I know who you are. Jesus, Joseph and Mary. I watched you grow up, young lady. Whatever you and my granddaughter were up to, I don't wanta know about it. Nothing but trouble, you kids. Now this, what they're saying. I never. Now you just scram."

Julia pushed back on the shutting door.

"Mrs. Davis, I have to talk to you."

"But I don't have to talk to you. You want me to call the police? I will."

Mrs. Davis tried again to shut the door, but Julia's foot kept it from closing.

"I'm here to help you, Mrs. Davis."

"I don't need any help."

"She's coming back."

Mrs. Davis stopped pushing against the door.

"You talked to her?"

"No. I just know her."

"You do, huh? You know she's crazy."

"Yes I do, Mrs. Davis. That's what I want to talk to you about. I think you might be in grave danger."

Mrs. Davis let out a sigh and opened the door.

"Oh, what the hell. You might as well come in."

Julia entered and looked around the dark living room. In the background she could hear a television from another room tuned to Nickelodeon, the children's channel.

"He sits in front of the TV all day and night. I think television should be treated like a controlled substance," said Mrs. Davis. "Kids get addicted to the damn thing."

"So do adults, Mrs. Davis."

"We can sit over here," said the elderly woman. She led Julia to a sofa on the far side of the small living room, far away from the doorway to the room with the television.

Julia sat on the sofa and Mrs. Davis took the easy chair next to it.

"I think Lizzie's gonna come here to get her son."

"That's a laugh. She don't care nothin for that boy. I been watchin' him since the day he was born. All Lizzie ever cared about was herself. Just like her mother. Apple didn't fall far from the tree that time. I usually start hearing from her mother bout this time."

"Lizzie told me her mother was dead."

"That's what she told everybody," said Mrs. Davis. "Got so she even started to believe it for a while."

"Why would she say something like that if it wasn't true?"

"I thought you said you knew Lizzie was crazy."

"I did."

"Well, then why'd you ask such a question? Lizzie ain't like other girls. Neither was her mother. Crazy as loons, both of them. Must have got it from the other side of the family. No insanity on my side far as I can tell."

"Her mother was insane?"

"Guess you didn't know my granddaughter as well as you thought."

"I know she's dangerous."

"That's the understatement of the year. They put her mother away for murder when Lizzie was still a child."

"Who'd she kill?"

"Her husband and her father. She woulda killed Lizzie too, but Lizzie was with me."

"What happened?"

"They'd all gone out celebrating. Lizzie's mom, her father and my husband Roy. Lizzie's grandfather," Mrs. Davis remembered aloud. "I stayed home and watched Lizzie. They all ended up at this motel, too drunk to drive. There was a fire. They found the bodies of the two men tied to the headboard of the bed. The prosecutor said Lizzie's mom had torched them. She claims she was innocent and the only reason she was blamed was because she was alive and they were dead. The prosecutor said evidence indicated there had been sexual intercourse and that Lizzie's mother had sex with one or both of the men in the bed. She's been in an institution for the criminally insane ever since. It just broke Lizzie's heart. She and her mother were so close, you see. Lizzie tried everything she could to get the verdict overturned. She got me to use my savings to hire detectives and doctors to dispute the evidence. It didn't work and the verdict stuck. Lizzie was devastated over not being able to help her mother."

Julia sighed and looked down at the floor. Then she looked up a Mrs. Davis.

"How old was Lizzie when this happened?" asked Julia.

"She was ten."

"She was 14 when I met her."

"By then she had gone to visit her mother a few times at the mental hospital. Then on one visit, Lizzie came out and she was crying and babbling about how her mother didn't recognize her. I went in to see what she was talking about and it was terrible. Her mother had aged twenty years. She looked older than me. Her beautiful brown hair had turned gray. Her face was white as a sheet and wrinkles had formed around her eyes. She was talking to herself and didn't even acknowledge my presence. We never went back and from then on, Lizzie talked as if her mother was dead."

"What would you do if Lizzie came back for Brian?" asked Julia.

"I wouldn't let her take him, that's for sure."

Mrs. Davis and Julia both looked across the room at Brian standing in the doorway to the room with the television.

"Hey baby," said Mrs. Davis. "Do you remember Mommy's friend, Julia?"

But Brian was crying.

Mrs. Davis got up and went to him. "How long have you been standing there?"

"I want Mommy," said Brian.

Mrs. Davis looked at Julia with pain in her eyes.

"I think I can help you," Julia said.

40

OFFICER LARSON was at his desk about to file his last report for the night when the operator beeped his phone. Larson. You got a call on line six.

He picked up the phone.

"It's Julia Stanton. You said to call if I needed any help."

"I sure did. What's up?"

"Well, I'm at the home of Lizzie Daly's grandmother. She's been taking care of Lizzie's son Brian. I just wondered if it would be possible to put a surveillance on her grandmother's house, but do it so nobody would know you were watching?"

"I doubt it, ma'am. We've been watching her house, your house, and the Daly residence for two weeks. I told you our situation. I wish I could do something about it but it's over my head that these decisions get made."

"Can I talk to the Chief, then?" asked Julia.

"What makes you so sure she'll come back now?"

"Because she would have been watching, too. Waiting for the police cars to leave."

"Well, wouldn't she keep doing that if they returned?" said Officer Larson. "Tell you what I'll do. Instead of planting an unmarked car there, I'll make sure somebody drives by once an hour and at different intervals. That way she won't be able to detect a pattern."

"That could work. Thanks," said Julia, and hung up.

Downtown Lakeside at night was lit up like any mid-sized American town. The Ostrich was doing a pretty good business tonight from the look of the overflow parking lot. A brand new black Jeep Grand Cherokee with tinted windows sat in the parking lot with the engine on. Slowly, the Jeep pulled out of its parking spot and drove down the street heading to the residential part of town.

The lights were off in Julia's house when the Jeep pulled up in front. The Jeep sat on the street next to the curb for about five minutes and then drove off. Two minutes later a police cruiser drove by slowly, its light splashed on the yard next to Julia's house, searching for any intruders.

Julia was looking out the front window when she saw a police cruiser drive by slowly. She backed away and joined Mrs. Davis in the kitchen and didn't see the Jeep Cherokee pull up across the street.

Mrs. Davis was stirring beef stew in a pot over a low flame on the kitchen stove.

"The secret to stew is the slow cooking. I hate these microwaves that make everything too hot to touch on the outside and keep everything frozen inside. It's unnatural. To cook right, you got to cook slow."

"Smells good, Mrs. Davis," said Julia. "I'm just gonna look in on Brian. I'll be right back."

"That won't be necessary," said Lizzie, who was standing in the doorway of the television room with her son Brian.

"Lizzie!"

"Hi Grandma. Julia. Just in time for supper."

"You get away from him," ordered Mrs. Davis.

"Who? My son?"

"How'd you get in here?"

"Well, I'm glad to see you, too. I need some money. Spent all I had on a new Jeep Cherokee. Those babies are expensive."

"What makes you think you can just walk in and start telling me what to do?"

"This."

Lizzie took out a gun and aimed it at Mrs. Davis.

"You'd shoot your own grandmother?"

"Only if you made me."

"Well, that's what you're gonna have to do if you think you're leaving here with that boy."

Lizzie looked down at Brian and then at her Grandmother. She shook her head as she brought up the pistol, cocking the hammer. "Oh, Grandma."

Before Lizzie could pull the trigger, Julia dove at her from the side, bringing her down like a linebacker tackling the quarterback in the middle of a pass.

Both women crashed to the floor and Lizzie dropped the gun. Lizzie turned and punched Julia in the face with her fist. Julia rolled away to avoid a second punch. Lizzie saw the gun lying against the wall. She started to crawl toward it, then reached out to pick it up when Julia pulled open a tote bag that was lying inside the doorway. She reached in and was about to pull something out when Lizzie came up with the gun in her hand.

Lizzie brought the gun around to aim at Julia when Julia leapt on Lizzie's back, forcing her down to the floor. Lizzie put her hands out in front to break the fall, but this time she didn't let go of the gun and it went off when she landed. The shot blew a hole in the wall next to Brian's head. Lizzie's eyes widened in terror when she saw how close she'd come to shooting her son.

"Goddamn you!" she screamed.

She tried to shake Julia off, but Julia put one of her knees down on the hand holding the gun. Julia then held up the hypodermic needle and plunged it into the back of Lizzie's hand, right in the area between the thumb and forefinger. The trigger finger.

Lizzie stared at the needle sticking out of the back of her hand. Julia pushed the plunger on the needle and Lizzie's hand shot open. The gun fell under the hand and the hand was limp at the wrist. "Agggghhh!" screamed Lizzie.

Using her other hand, Lizzie backslapped Julia across the face. She then yanked the needle out of her hand and stood up. Julia pushed away from the floor as Lizzie reached down to pick up the gun. She tried to steady herself and the gun as she came up aiming the gun at Julia.

"No!" screamed Mrs. Davis.

Lizzie tried to pull the trigger, but she couldn't make her finger move.

"My hand," said Lizzie. "It's numb."

"As an oral hygienist, I'm not allowed to administer novocaine since it's considered an anesthetic. But what the hell. I don't think they'll hold it against me this time, do you? Works pretty fast, don't it?"

Suddenly, an idea registered in Lizzie's face and she started to switch hands but Julia reached out faster and took the gun out of her frozen hand. Now Julia held the gun on Lizzie.

"Okay. You win. Now finish it."

"It is finished. Mrs. Davis. Call the police."

"I'm not gonna spend the rest of my life in jail. I'd rather be dead. Come on, Julia. Do it."

"No."

"In that case, I'm leaving."

Lizzie started for the door when Brian ran over to block her way.

"Mommy," pleaded Brian.

Lizzie looked down at her son. "Oh Brian. I'm sorry."

"Don't go Mommy."

Lizzie felt her eyes watering as she looked down at her son. She raised her head and looked at Julia and her grandmother. Tears were rolling down Lizzie's face as her son grabbed her leg and hugged his mother.

Lizzie reached down and picked up her son. "You want to come with Mommy?"

"Put him down!" ordered Julia.

"Or what, you'll shoot? I don't think so."

Lizzie turned and opened the door. She was about to step outside when she saw the three police cars, their lights flashing, parked around her black Jeep. Office Larson was on one knee in the middle of the lawn, his revolver drawn and aimed at Lizzie.

"Freeze!"

Julia moved to the doorway.

"It's okay," screamed Julia. "She's not armed."

Julia gave Grandma Davis the gun.

Officer Larson put his pistol away and approached the women in the doorway. "One of the patrol units spotted the black Jeep and called it in. Mrs. Daly, I'm afraid I'm going to have to place you under arrest."

Lizzie nodded and then looked at her son. "You go with Grandma now, okay? Just remember what I said about nightmares. If they ever get too bad, just wake yourself up and they'll all go away."

As Larson locked the handcuffs on Lizzie, she turned toward Julia.

"Hey, hot stuff."

Julia stiffened.

"Do me a favor, will ya?"

"I'll try," said Julia.

"Look in on Brian for me, will ya? That old bird will spoil that boy. Besides. It'll give you some practice for when you finally get one of your own."

"Sure."

Larson led Lizzie away as Julia watched from the doorway. It was finally over. She wondered why she didn't feel better. Then the realization hit her. It wasn't really over. She just needed to give herself a little more time.

41

LIZZIE THOUGHT it was a bit much that they had to keep her handcuffed by one hand to her hospital bed. I mean, where did they think she was going to go, anyway? Do they realize how uncomfortable this is? What if I get a cramp? I could sue them. I guess it's better than a jail cell. Have to remember to thank Julia for giving me that shot of novocaine. Good thing she didn't know I'd have an allergic reaction that required hospitalization. Oh well, might as well make the best use of this.

Lizzie shifted as much as she could in the hospital bed while still being handcuffed to the headboard. She looked relatively healthy and appeared to be reading several thick law books that were spread out on the bed around her.

A guard sat just outside her door reading *People* magazine. Lizzie closed a book and picked up the phone with her one free hand. She punched in a number.

"Mr. Bender, please," said Lizzie into the phone. "This is Lizzie Daly. He's expecting my call."

"Mrs. Daly," said a male voice over the phone. "Patrick Bender here. I've been reviewing your case."

"Good. Whatta ya think?"

"Considering your family history, I'd say we had a fairly reasonable chance for an insanity plea. We might even be able to build a case to have you sentenced to the same facility as your mother. Especially if we can convince the psychiatric community it would assist in your rehabilitation."

Lizzie picked up a photo of a little girl with a young woman. The young girl looked like a young Lizzie, and so did the young woman.

"Mrs. Daly? Are you there?"

"I'm here."

"Did you hear what I said? About serving your sentence with your mother?"

"Hey. That's why you make them big bucks."

"Speaking of money, Mrs. Daly. I'm going to need a retainer before I start filing motions."

"A retainer, huh? I'm a little short in the cash flow department Mr. Bender."

"Well, you must have some assets that could be liquidated."

"Would you accept a ring?"

"A ring?"

"It's a family heirloom, actually. Gold with diamond inlays. It should appraise at about twenty thousand dollars. How's that sound?"

"That should cover it."

"Goodbye then Mr. Bender."

Lizzie hung up the phone. She lifted the photo to her lips and kissed it.

"See you soon, Momma."

Four months had passed and Bruce's stitches had long since healed. But it still hurt a little to run, so he had to walk after the wiffle ball his daughter had just smacked into a neighbor's yard. As he bent down and picked up the small plastic white ball, he saw the old Buick moving slowly down the street toward his house.

Who could this be? The car looked familiar. It had Connecticut plates. Suddenly, a big smile broke across Bruce's face as the car stopped and Julia Stanton climbed out. She was wearing her oral hygienist uniform, but Bruce didn't care. As far as he was concerned, she was the most beautiful woman in the world.

Julia walked across the lawn to Bruce and gave him a big hug. She then felt the eyes of the young girl and turned around and knelt down on one knee.

"You must be Lisa," said Julia to the little girl with a yellow wiffle bat over her shoulder.

"Are you the lady who saved Daddy's life?" asked Lisa.

Julia looked up at Bruce and smiled a tearful smile.

"No, Lisa. You are."

FRED YAGER is a business television executive and screenwriter. He was a reporter for the Associated Press for 13 years covering everything from Watergate and entertainment to general reporting and crime. He has also worked at CBS News and Fox Television. A member of the Writers Guild of America, several of his screenplays have been optioned.

JAN YAGER (www.janyager.com) has a doctorate in sociology (City University of New York, 1983), an MA in criminal justice, and is the author of numerous nonfiction books including *Victims*. A member of the American Society of Criminology and Mystery Writers of America, she has taught criminology at The New School and Temple University and writing at Penn State.

JUST YOUR EVERYDAY PEOPLE is the second suspense novel co-authored by Fred Yager and his wife Jan Yager (the former Janet Barkas). *UNTIMELY DEATH* (Hannacroix Creek Books, 1998, Swedish edition, Kentaur Press, 2000), also a suspense novel, was their first co-authored novel.

www.ingramcontent.com/pod-product-compliance
Lightning Source LLC
Chambersburg PA
CBHW050409260626
47156CB00003B/931